Box

BOX (Book One) © 2019 Patrick Wirbeleit & Uwe Heidschötter.

Originally published by Reprodukt (Germany) in 2014.
Rights arranged through Nicolas Grivel Agency.
English Translation © Peta Devlin.

ISBN: 978-1-60309-449-8   23 22 21 20 19   5 4 3 2 1

Published by Top Shelf Productions, PO Box 1282, Marietta, GA 30061-1282, USA.
Top Shelf Productions is an imprint of IDW Publishing, a division of Idea and
Design Works, LLC. Offices: 2765 Truxtun Road, San Diego, CA 92106. Top Shelf
Productions®, the Top Shelf logo, Idea and Design Works®, and the IDW logo
are registered trademarks of Idea and Design Works, LLC. All Rights Reserved.
With the exception of small excerpts of artwork used for review purposes, none of
the contents of this publication may be reprinted without the permission of IDW
Publishing. IDW Publishing does not read or accept unsolicited submissions of ideas,
stories or artwork.

Printed in Korea.

Editor-in-Chief: Chris Staros.

Designed by Gilberto Lazcano.

Visit our online catalog at topshelfcomix.com.

Uwe Heidschötter

Box

top
Shelf
PRODUCTIONS

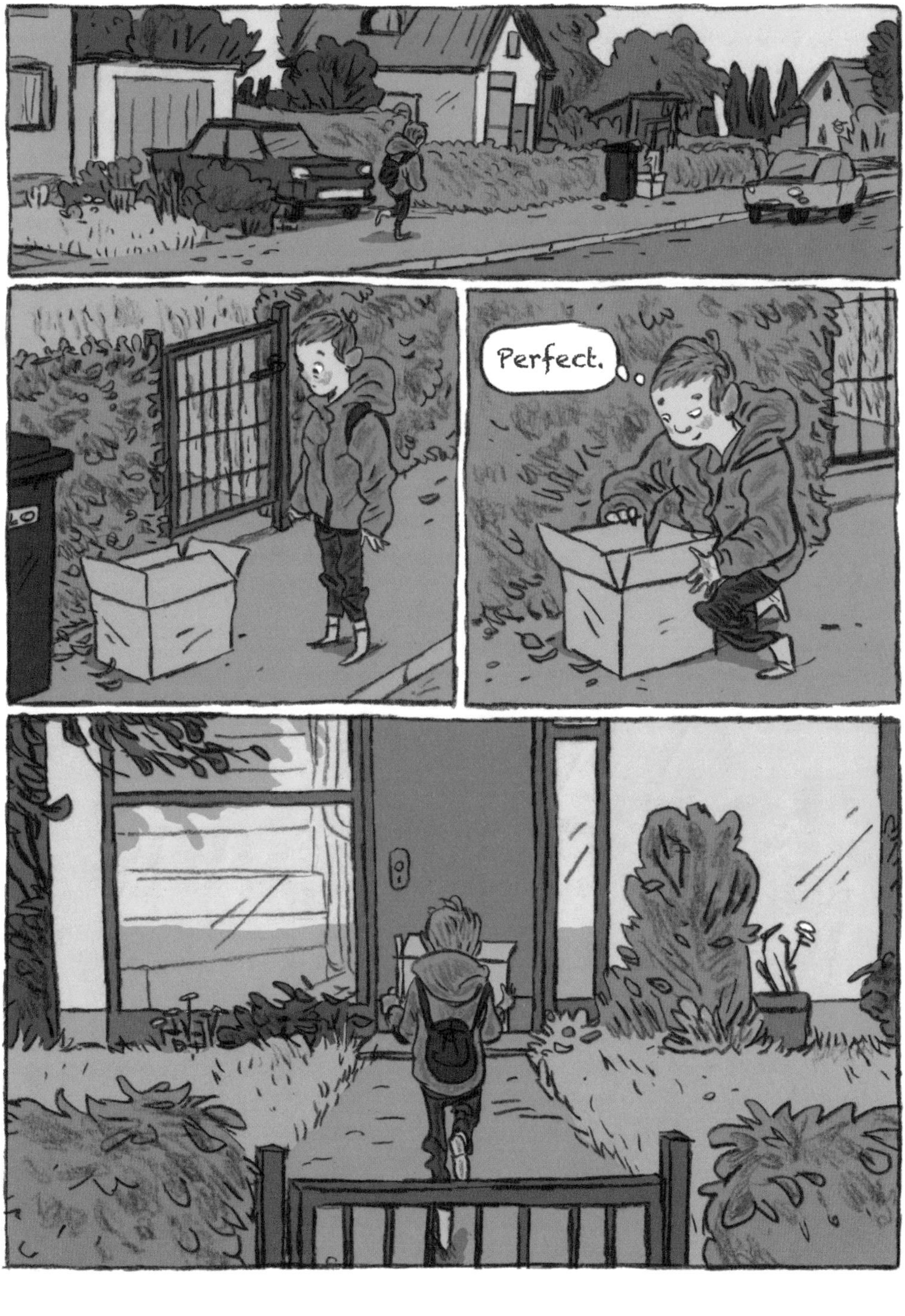
Perfect.

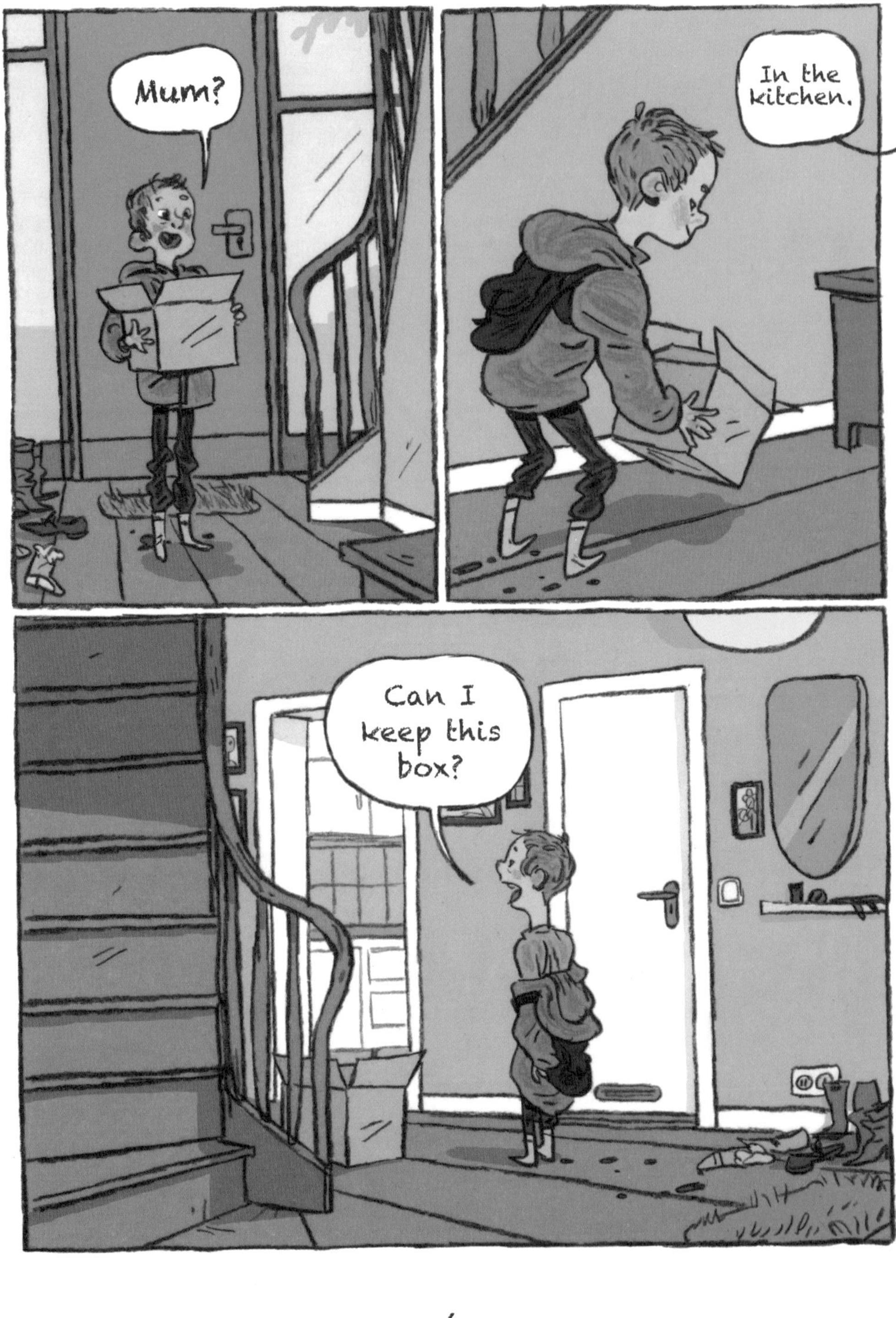
Mum?
In the kitchen.
Can I keep this box?

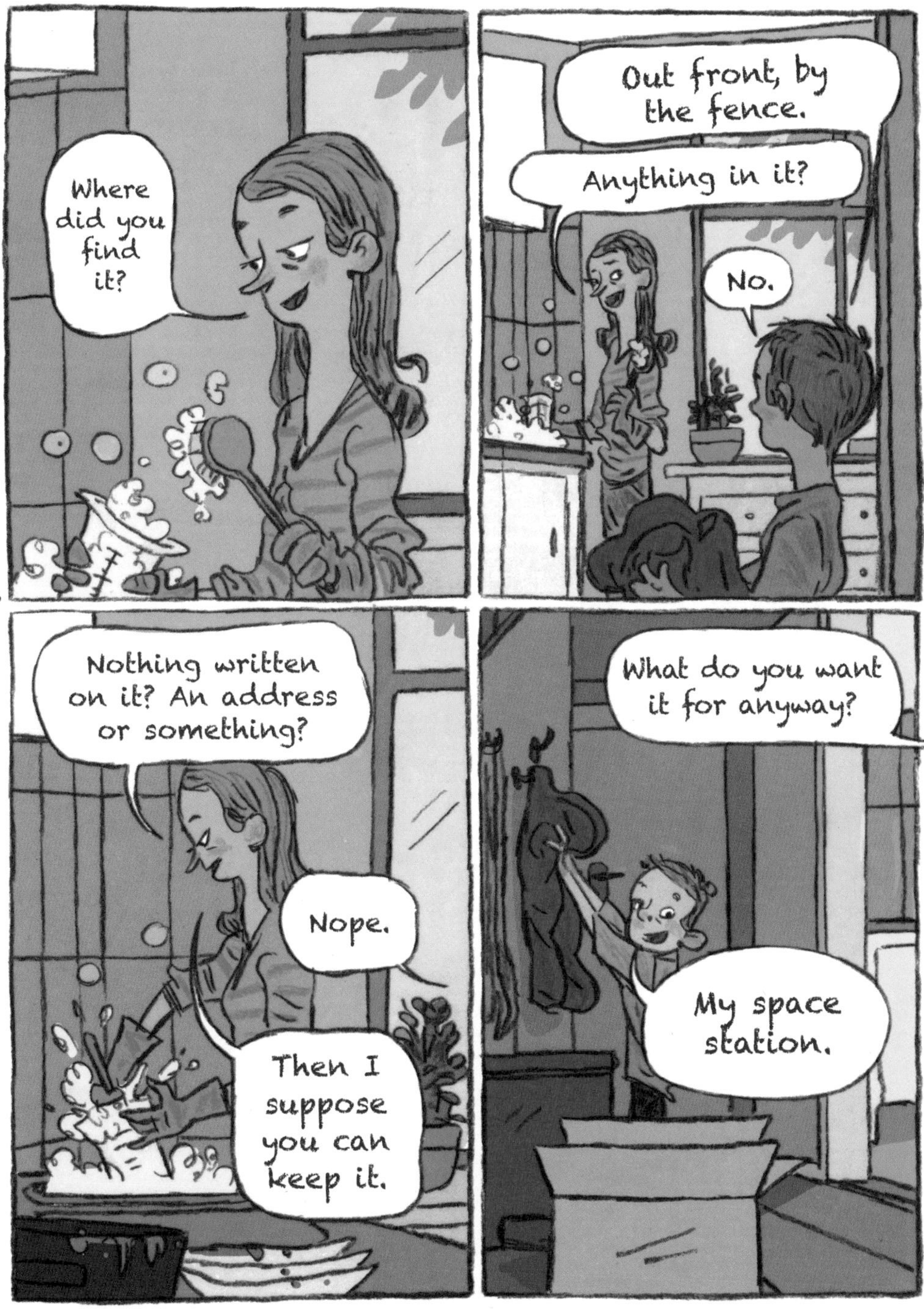
Where did you find it?
Out front, by the fence.
Anything in it?
No.
Nothing written on it? An address or something?
Nope.
Then I suppose you can keep it.
What do you want it for anyway?
My space station.

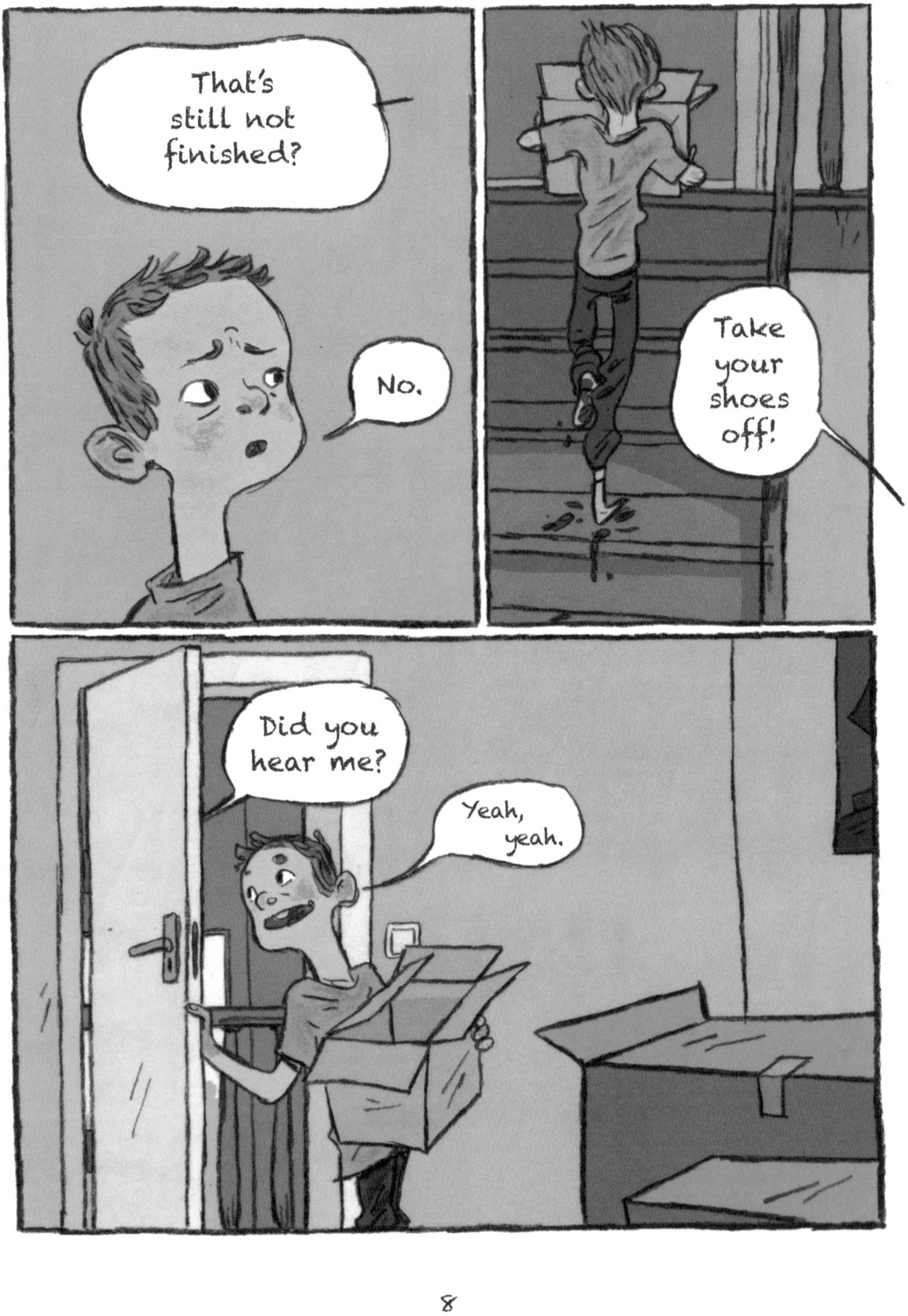
That's still not finished?
No.
Take your shoes off!
Did you hear me?
Yeah, yeah.

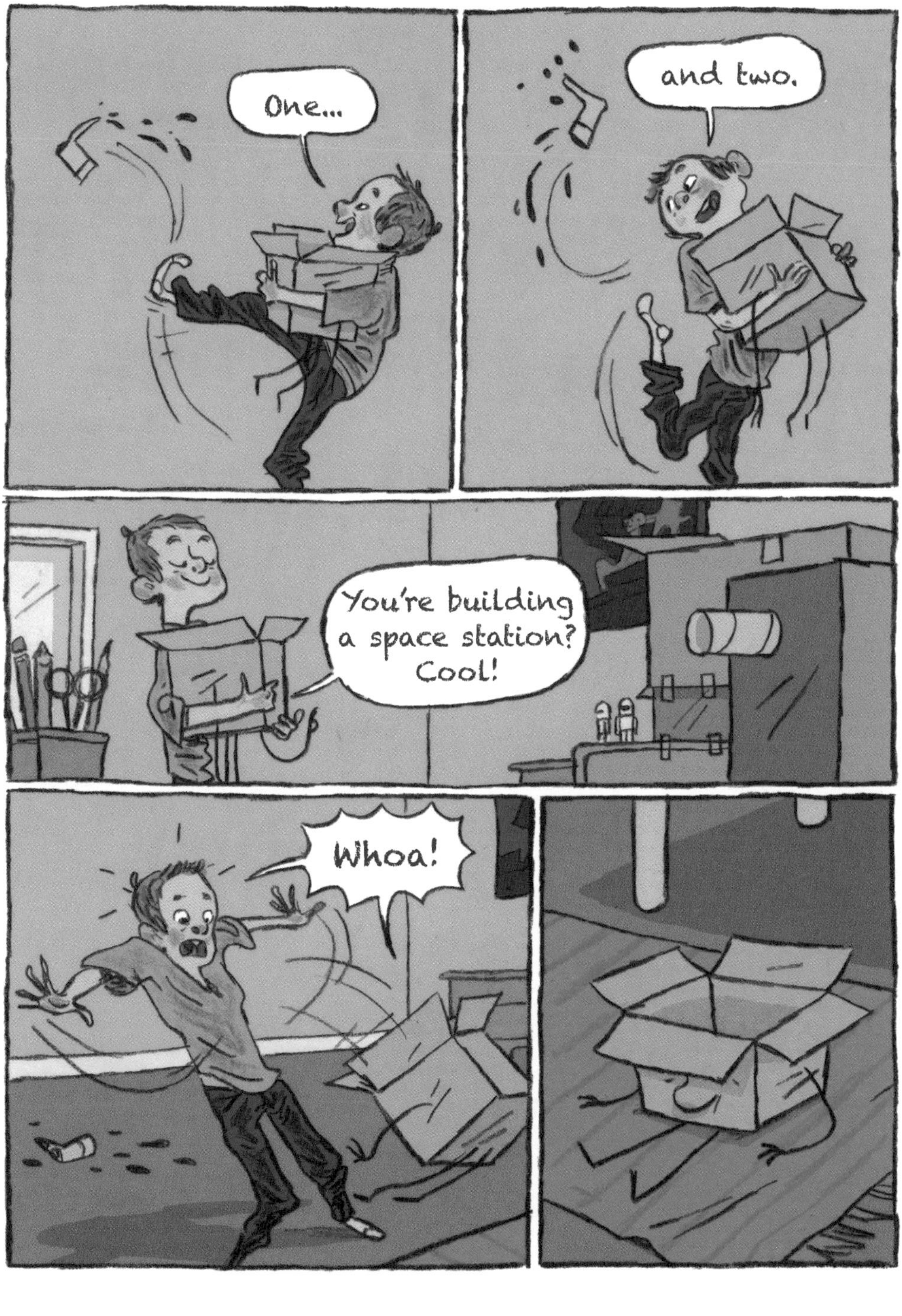
One...
and two.
You're building a space station? Cool!
Whoa!

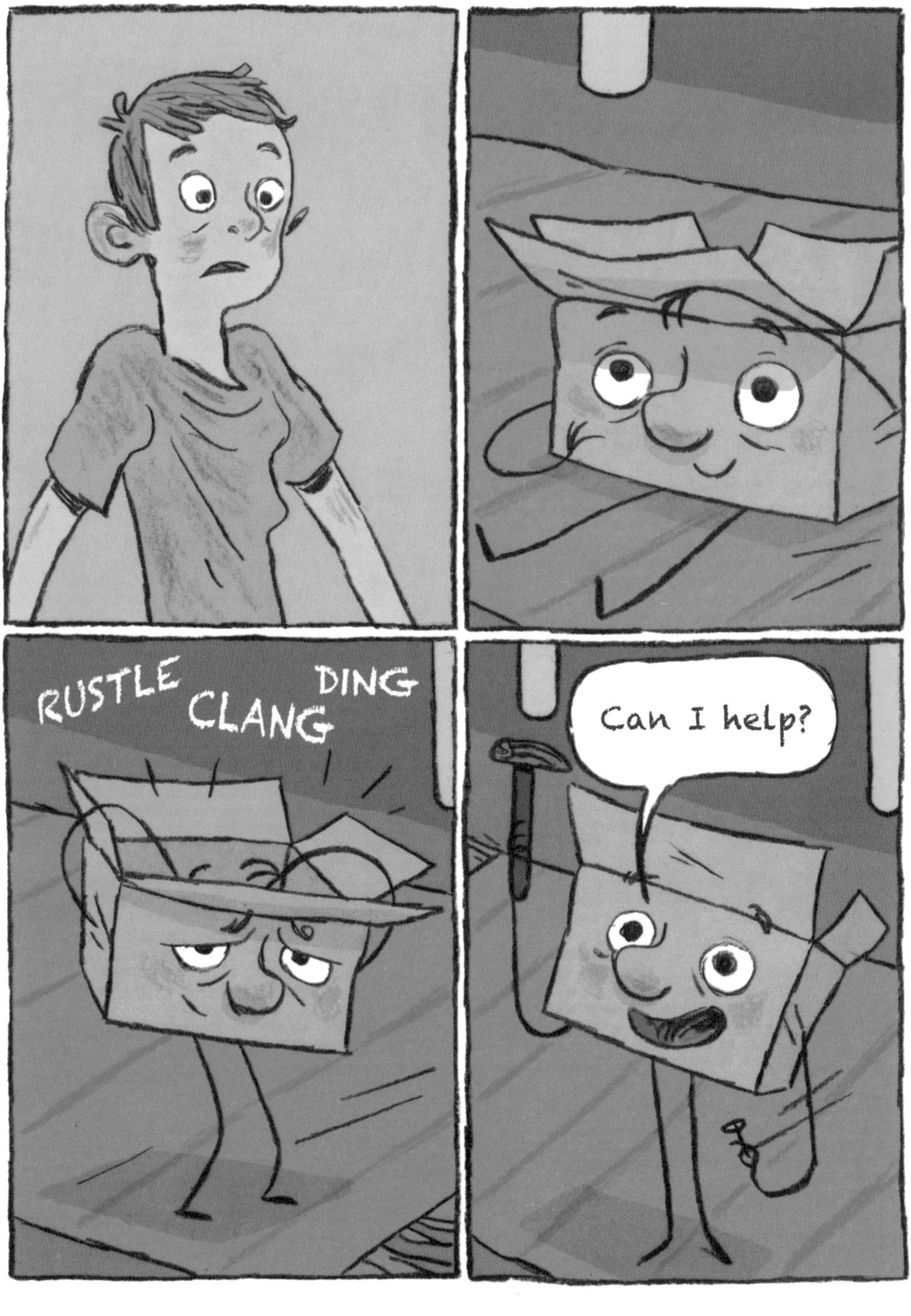
RUSTLE
CLANG
DING
Can I help?

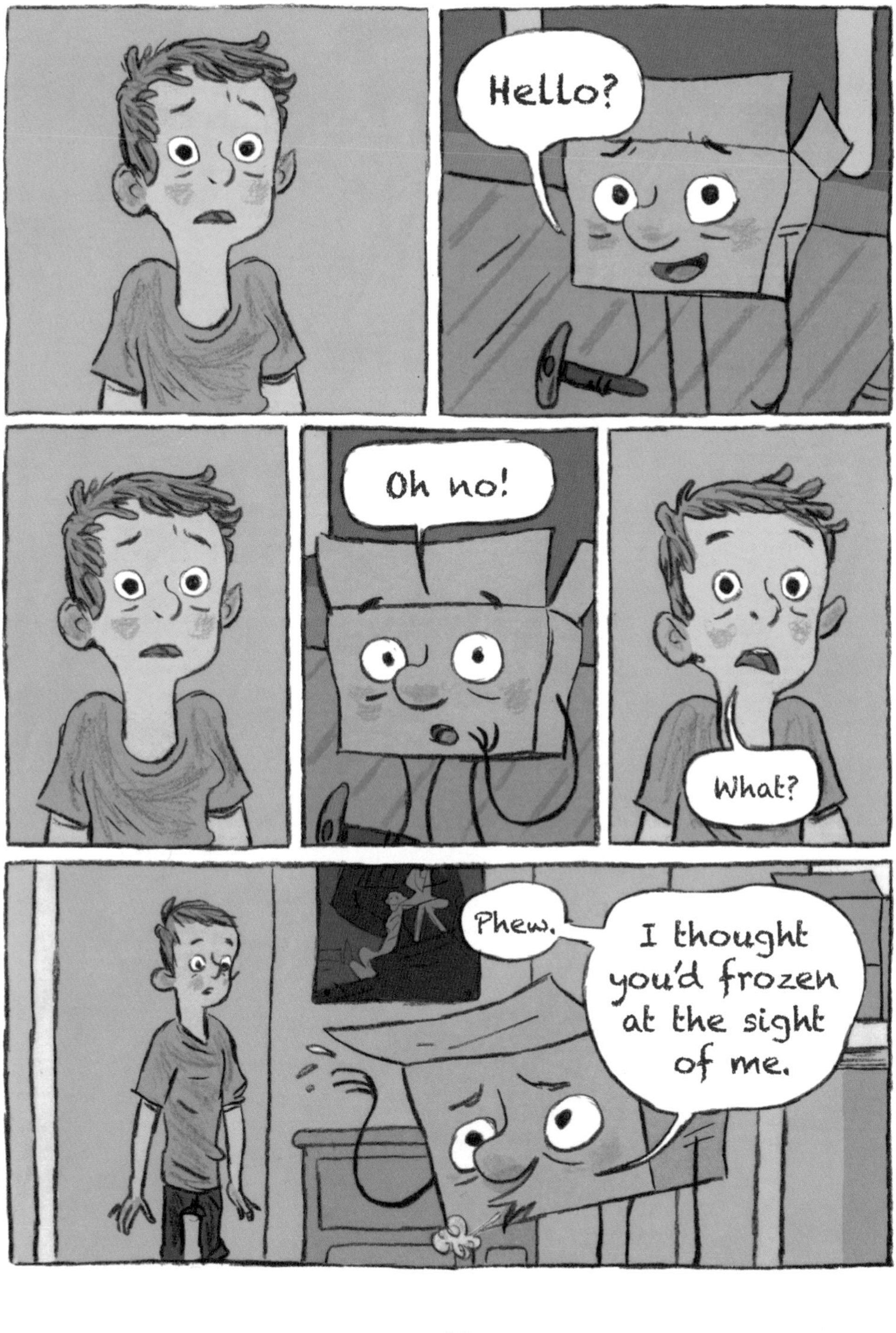
Hello?
Oh no!
What?
Phew.
I thought you'd frozen at the sight of me.

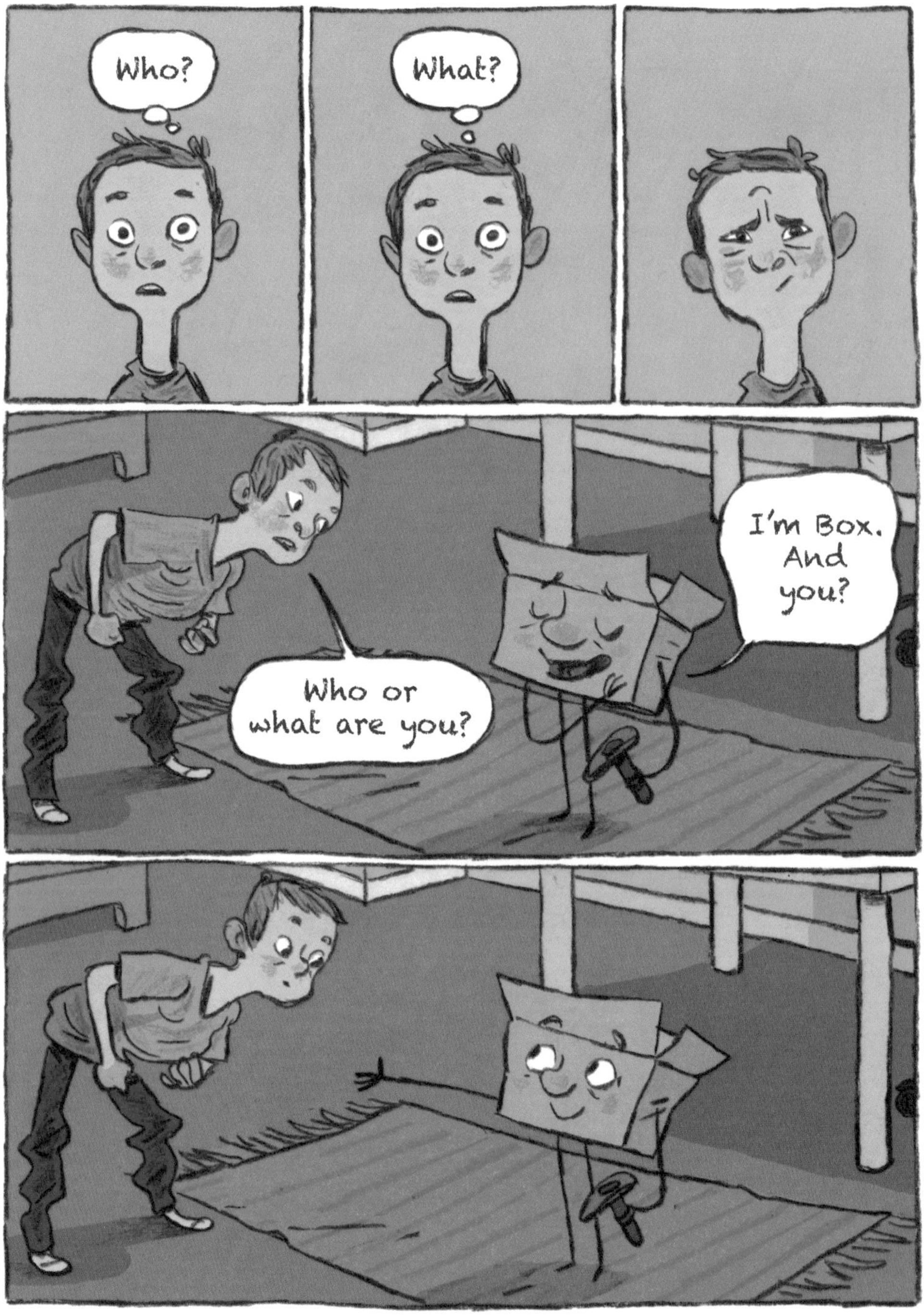
Who?
What?
Who or
what are you?
I'm Box.
And
you?

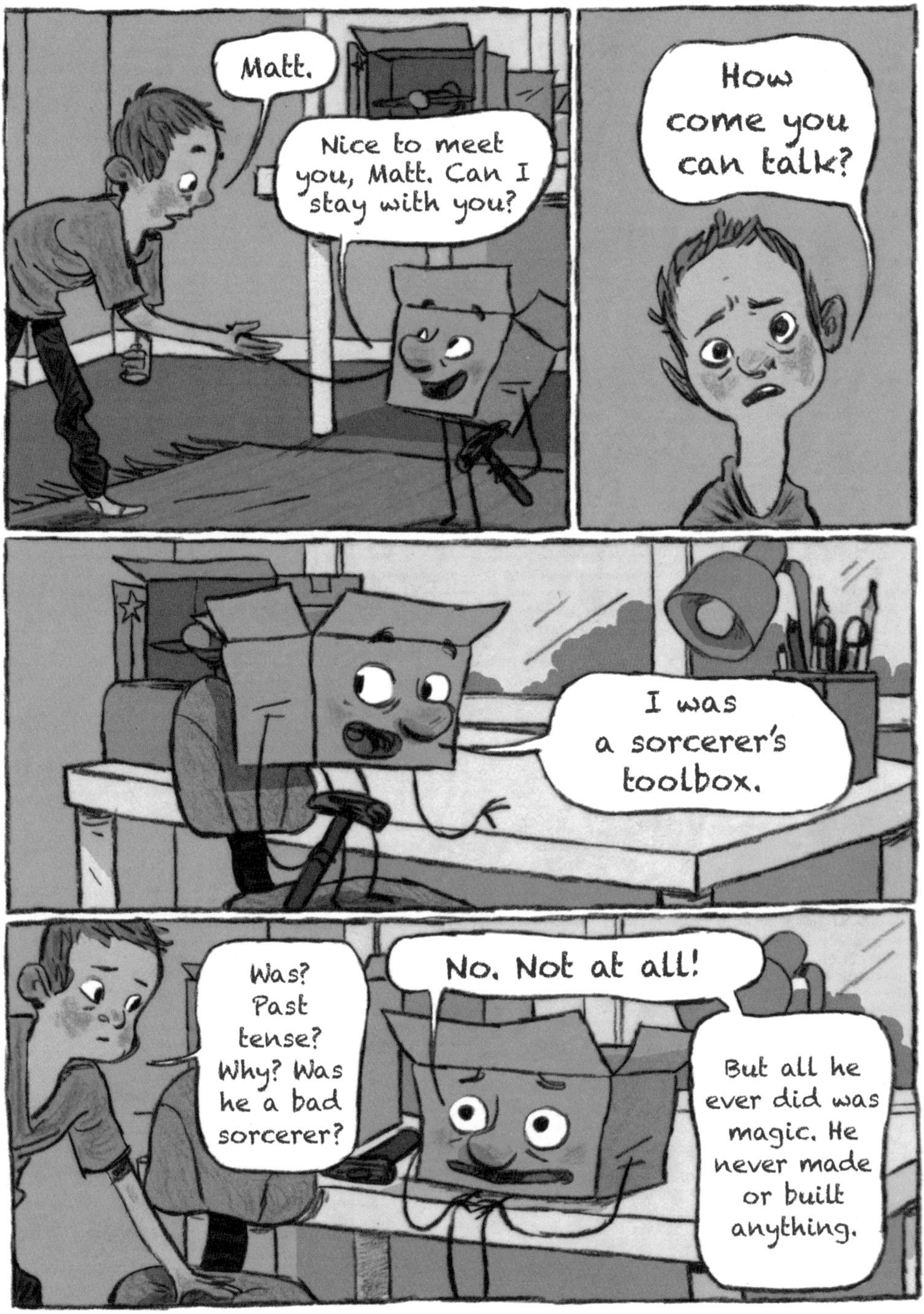
Matt.
Nice to meet you, Matt. Can I stay with you?
How come you can talk?
I was a sorcerer's toolbox.
Was? Past tense? Why? Was he a bad sorcerer?
No. Not at all!
But all he ever did was magic. He never made or built anything.

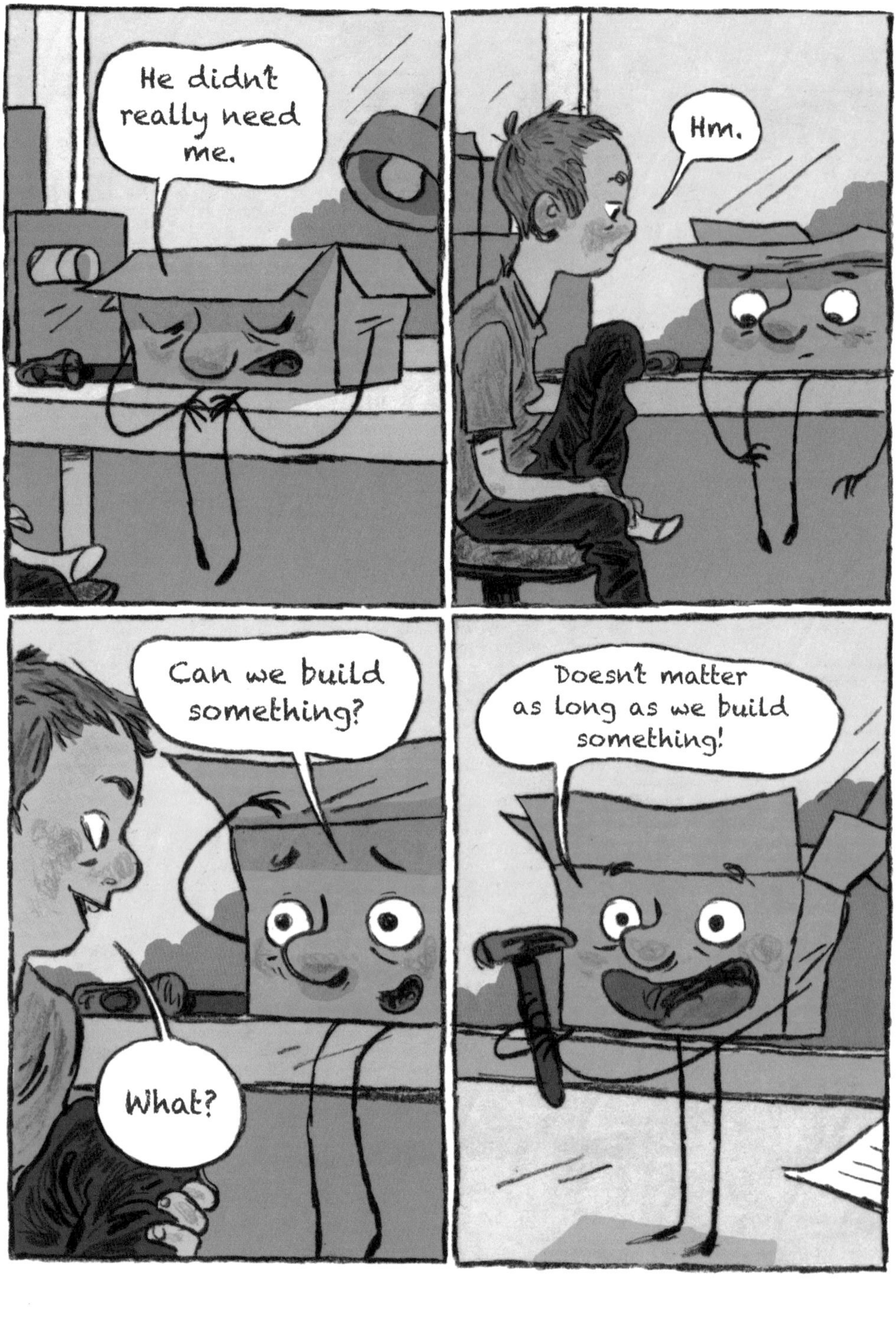
He didn't really need me.
Hm.
Can we build something?
What?
Doesn't matter as long as we build something!

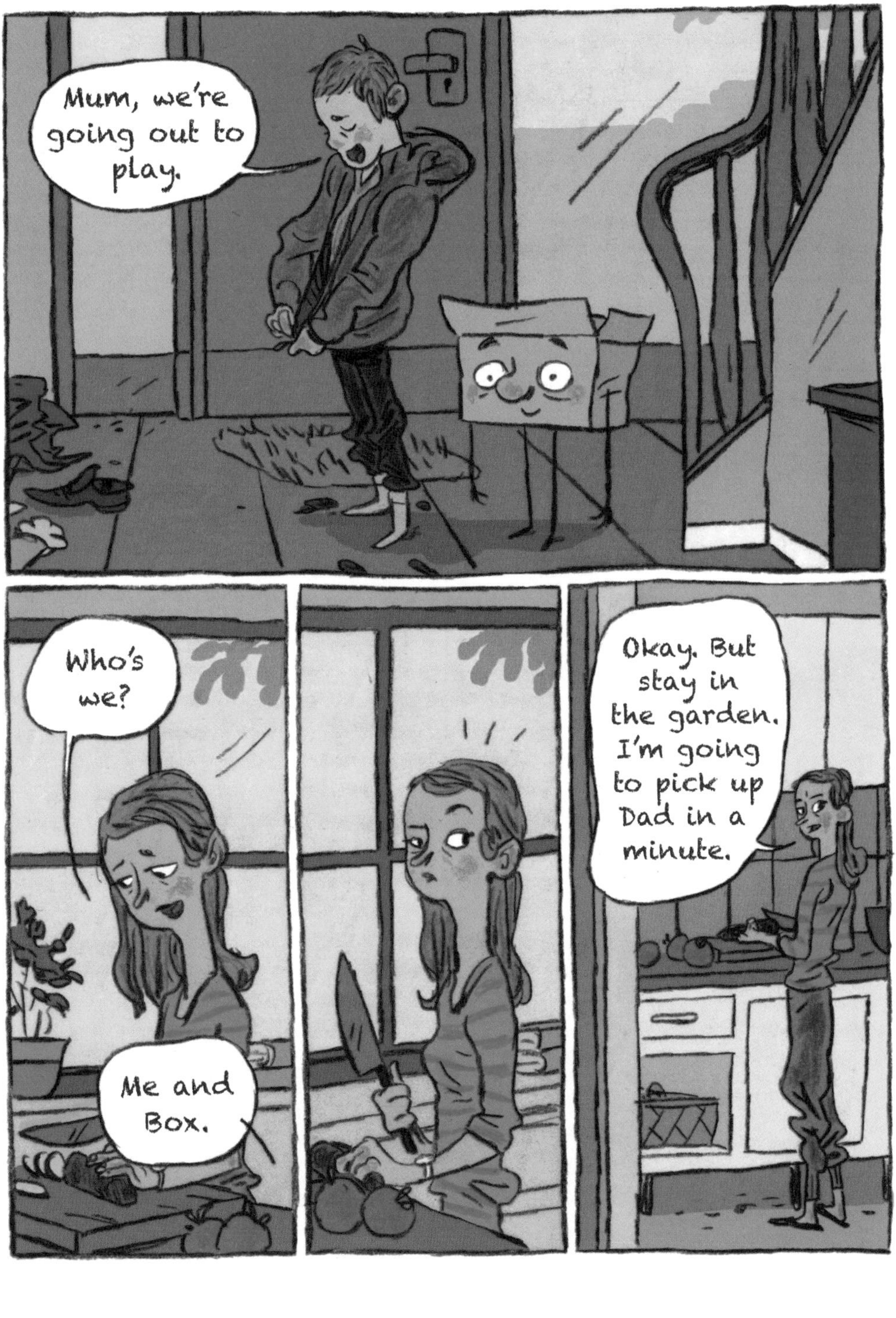
Mum, we're going out to play.
Who's we?
Me and Box.
Okay. But stay in the garden. I'm going to pick up Dad in a minute.

The See-Saw

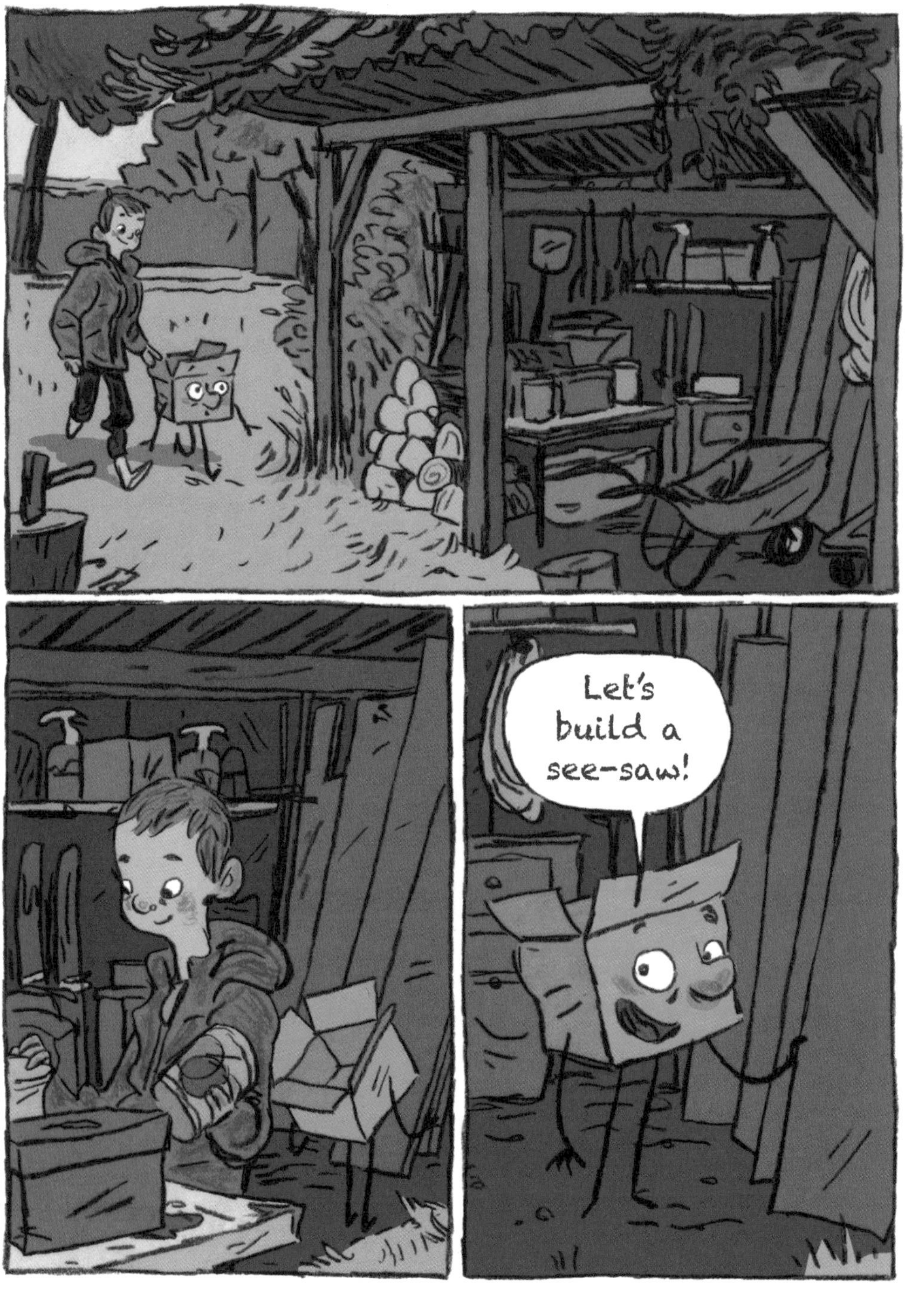
Let's
build a
see-saw!

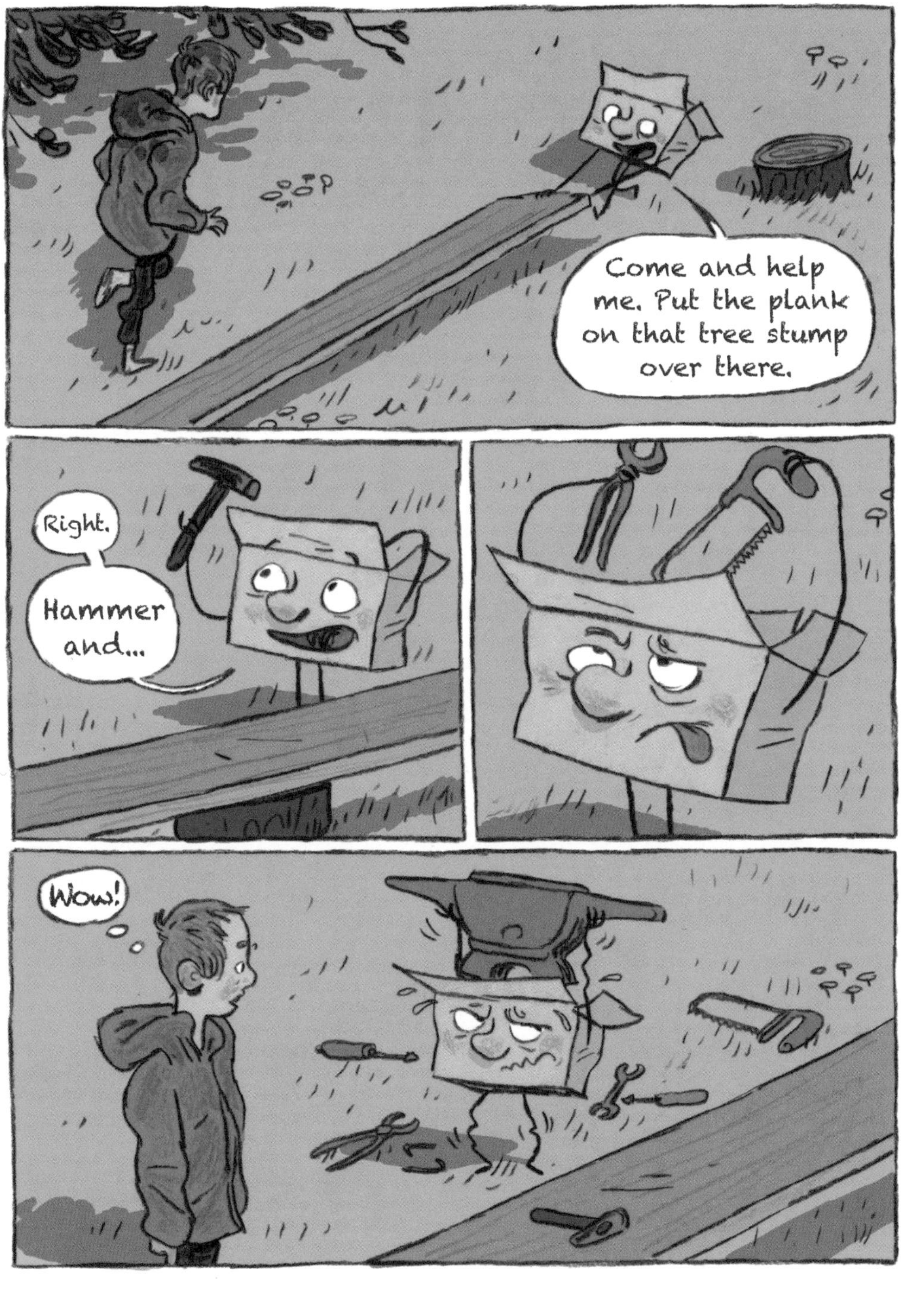
Come and help me. Put the plank on that tree stump over there.
Right.
Hammer and...
Wow!

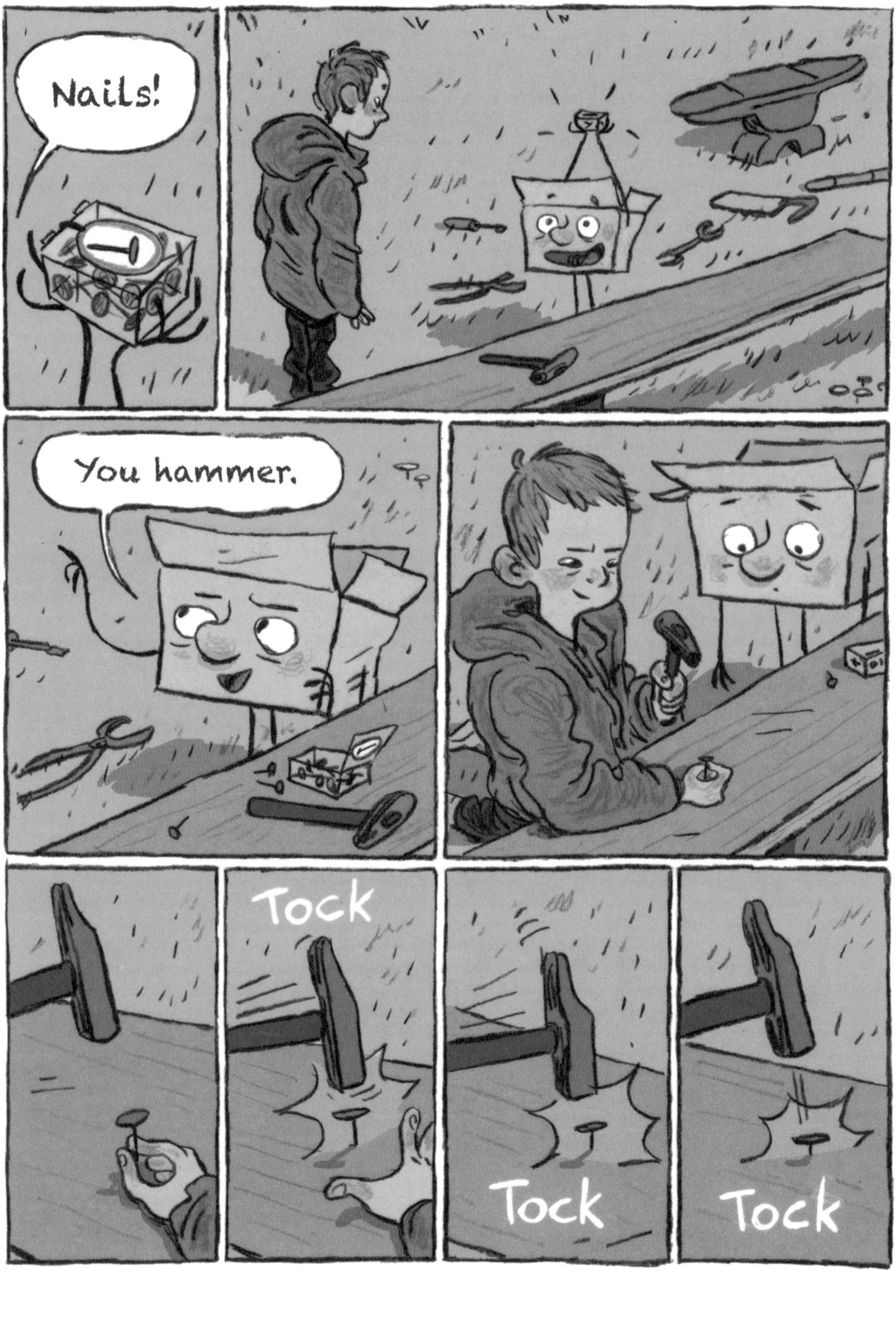
Nails!
You hammer.
Tock
Tock
Tock

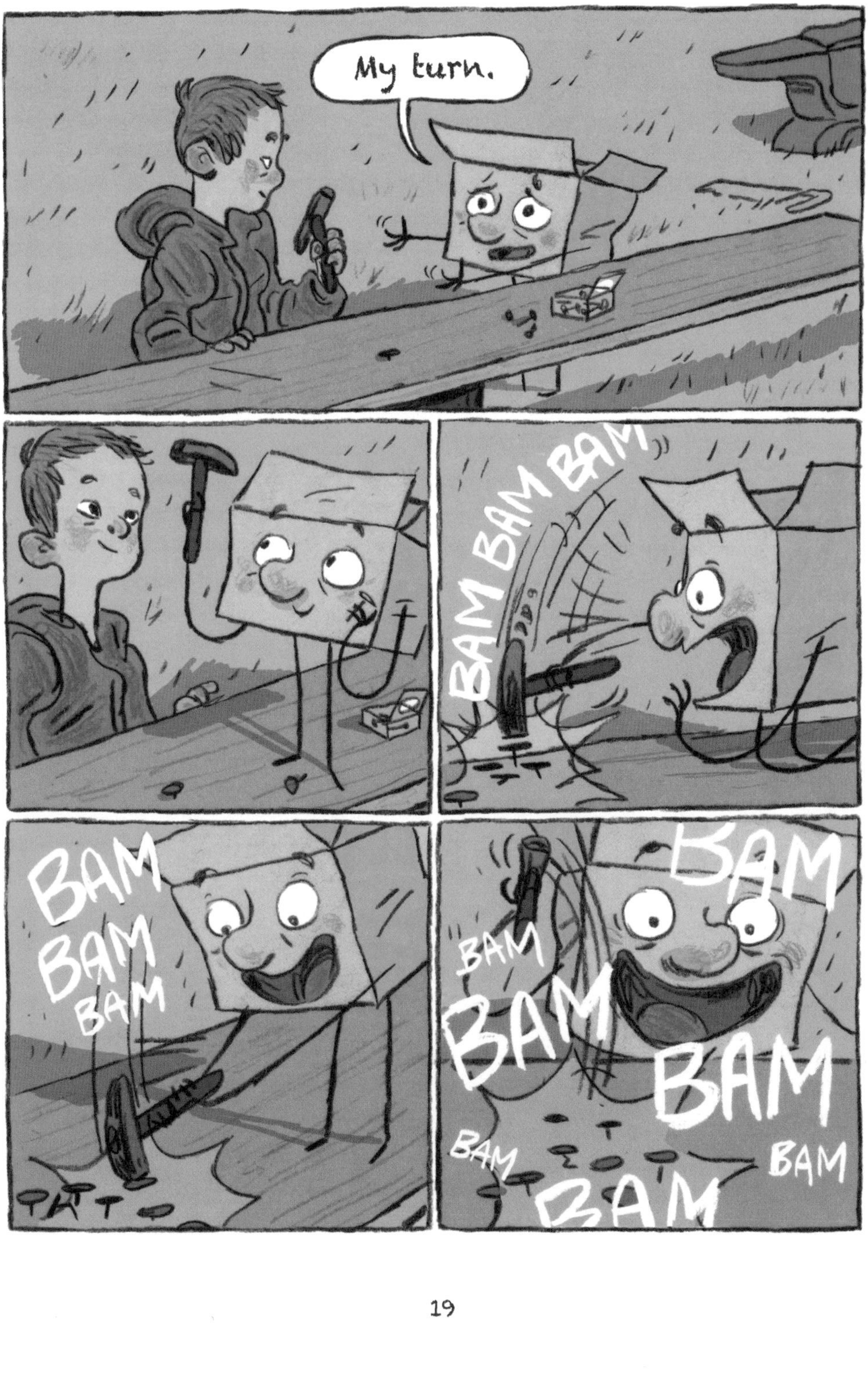
My turn.
BAM BAM BAM BAM
BAM
BAM
BAM
BAM
BAM
BAM
BAM
BAM
BAM
BAM

Come on...
let's
see-saw!
But
you can't
see-saw
on that.
You can,
you can!
Oh.
It's obvious why
it won't see-saw. You
have to get on the
other end first.

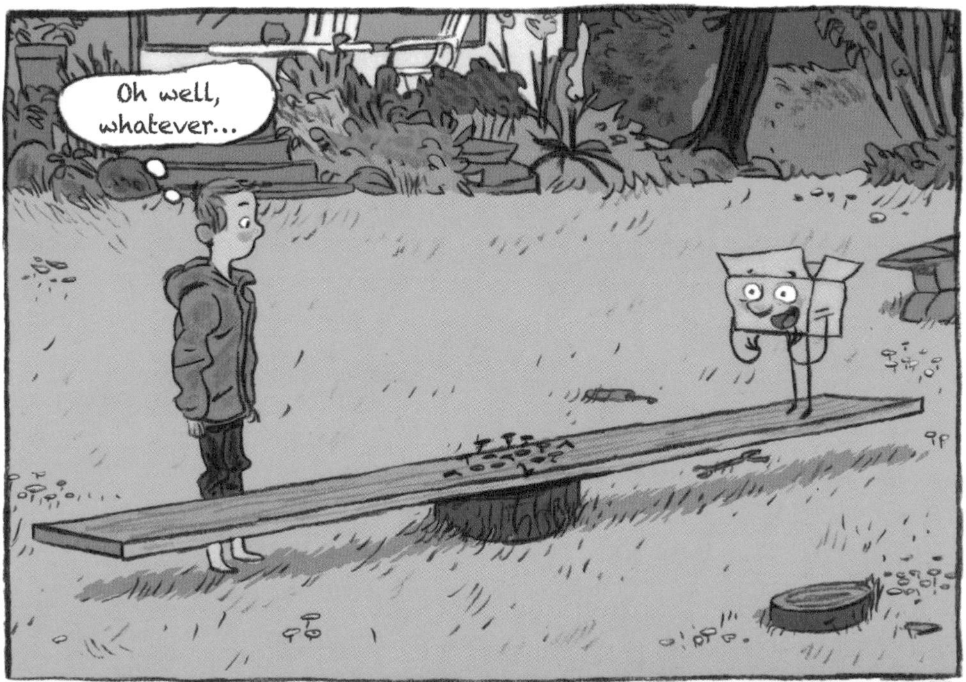
Oh well, whatever...

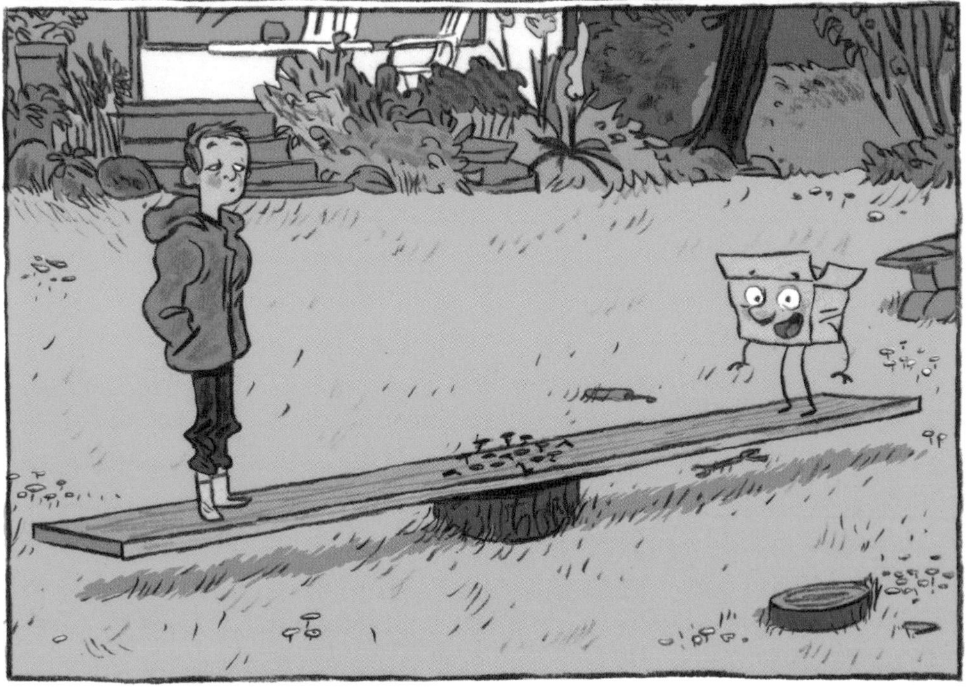

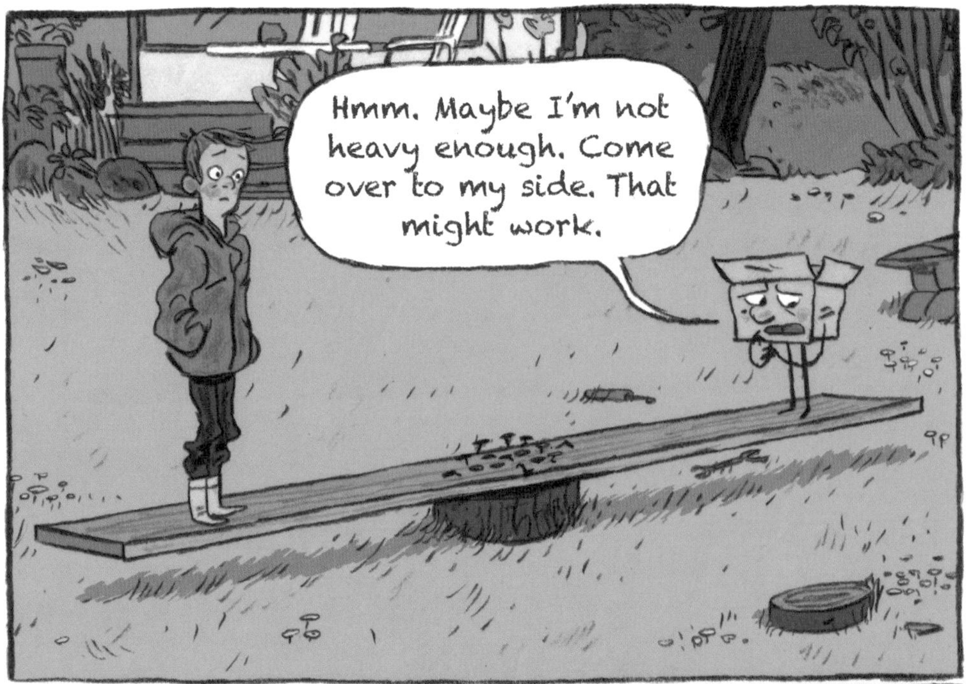
Hmm. Maybe I'm not heavy enough. Come over to my side. That might work.

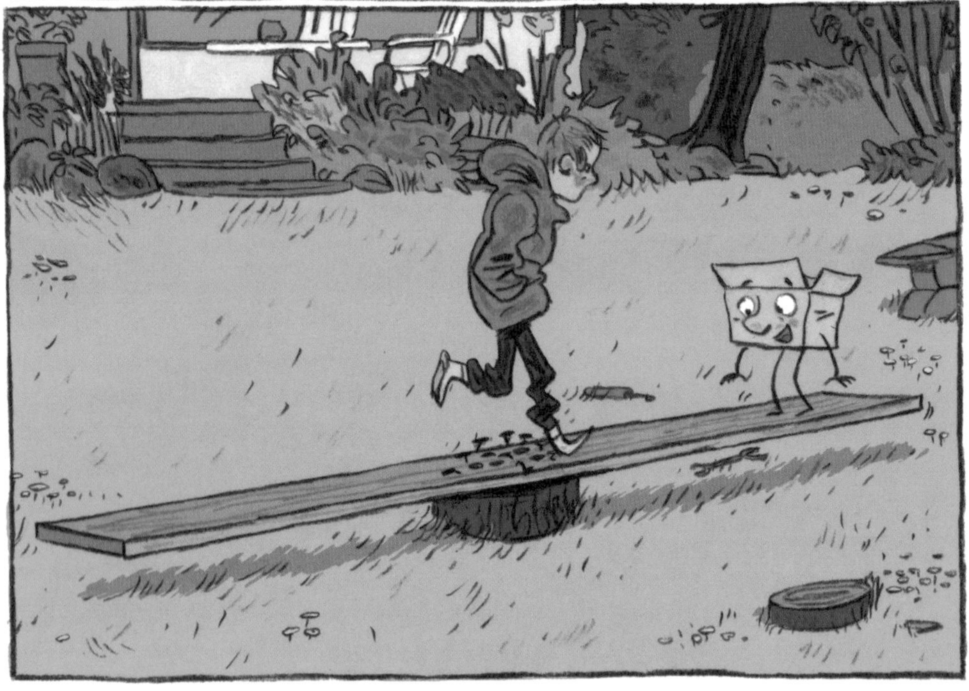

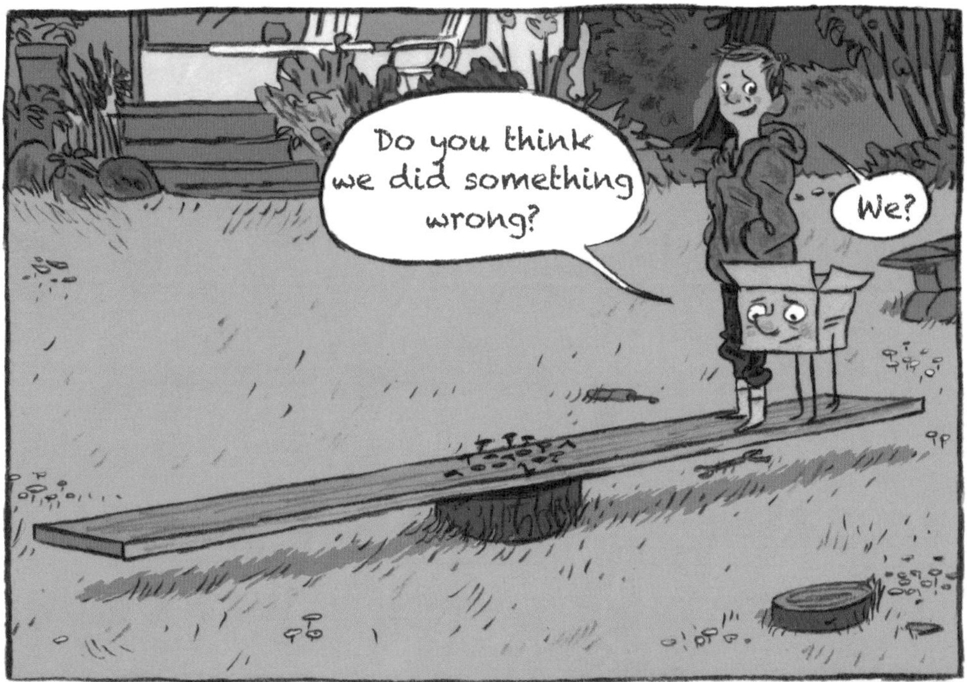
Do you think we did something wrong?
We?

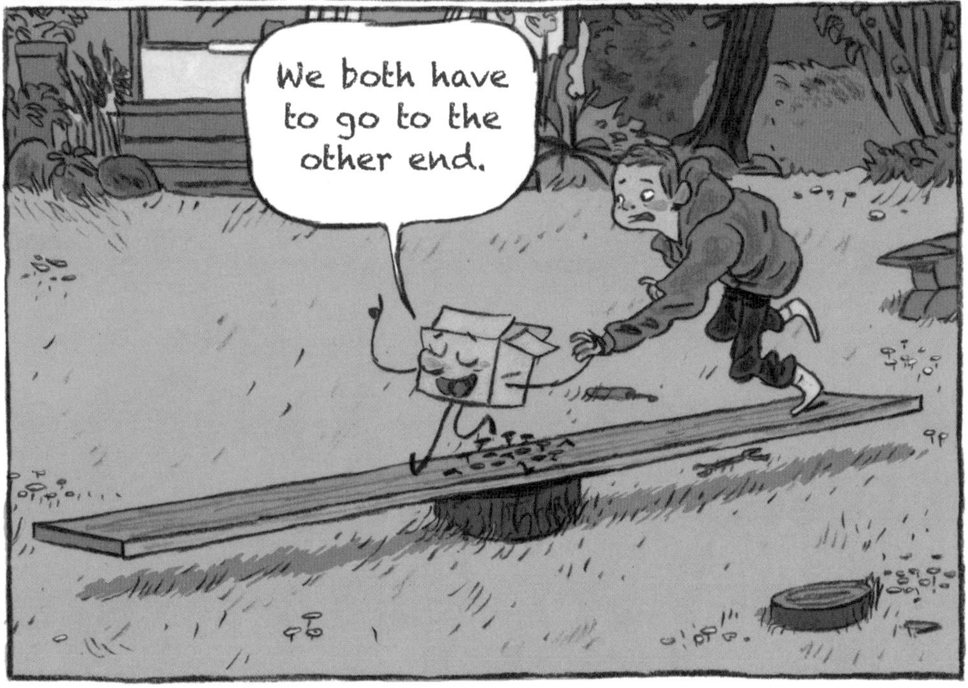
We both have to go to the other end.

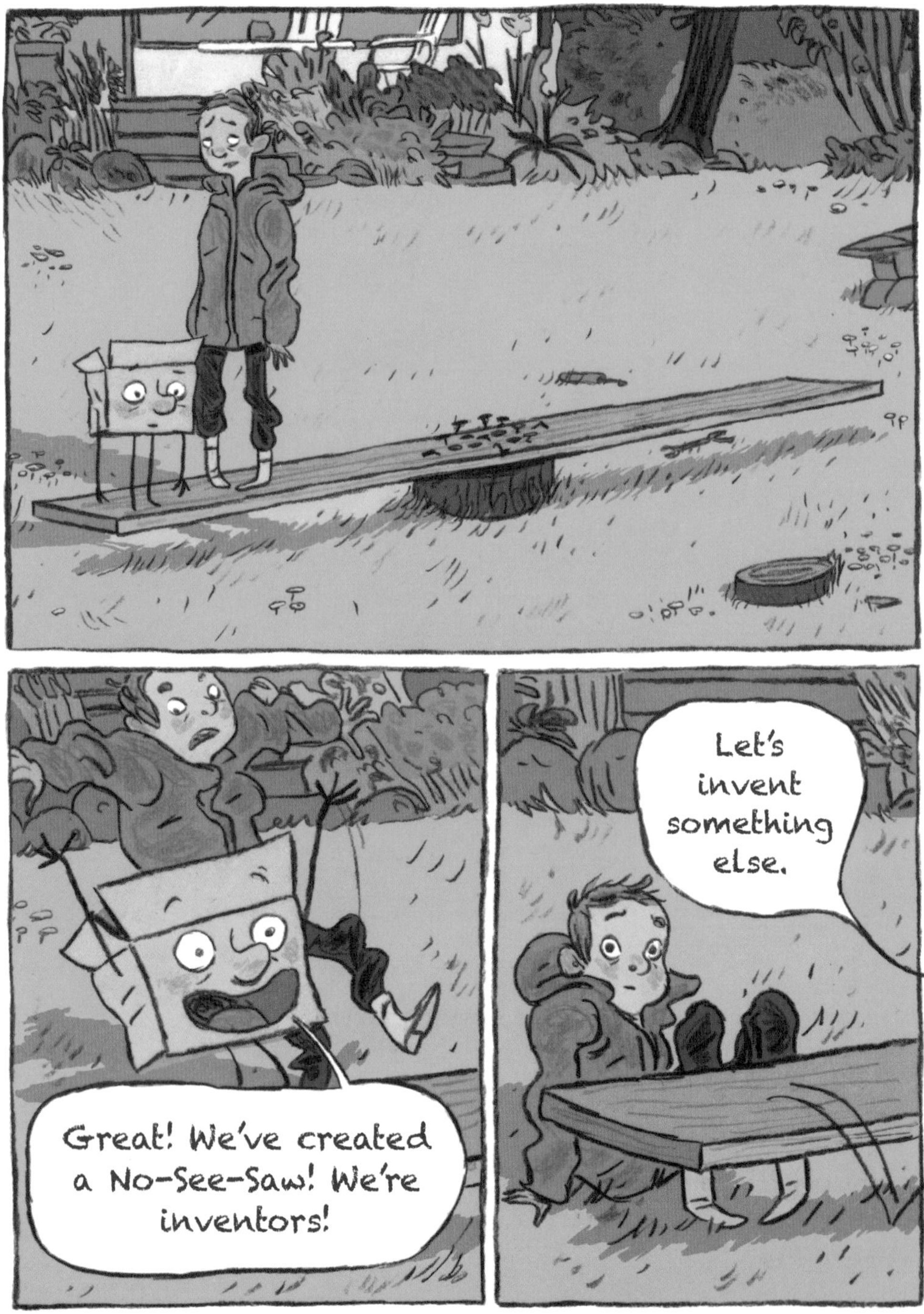
Great! We've created a No-See-Saw! We're inventors!
Let's invent something else.

The What-Happens-Then Machine

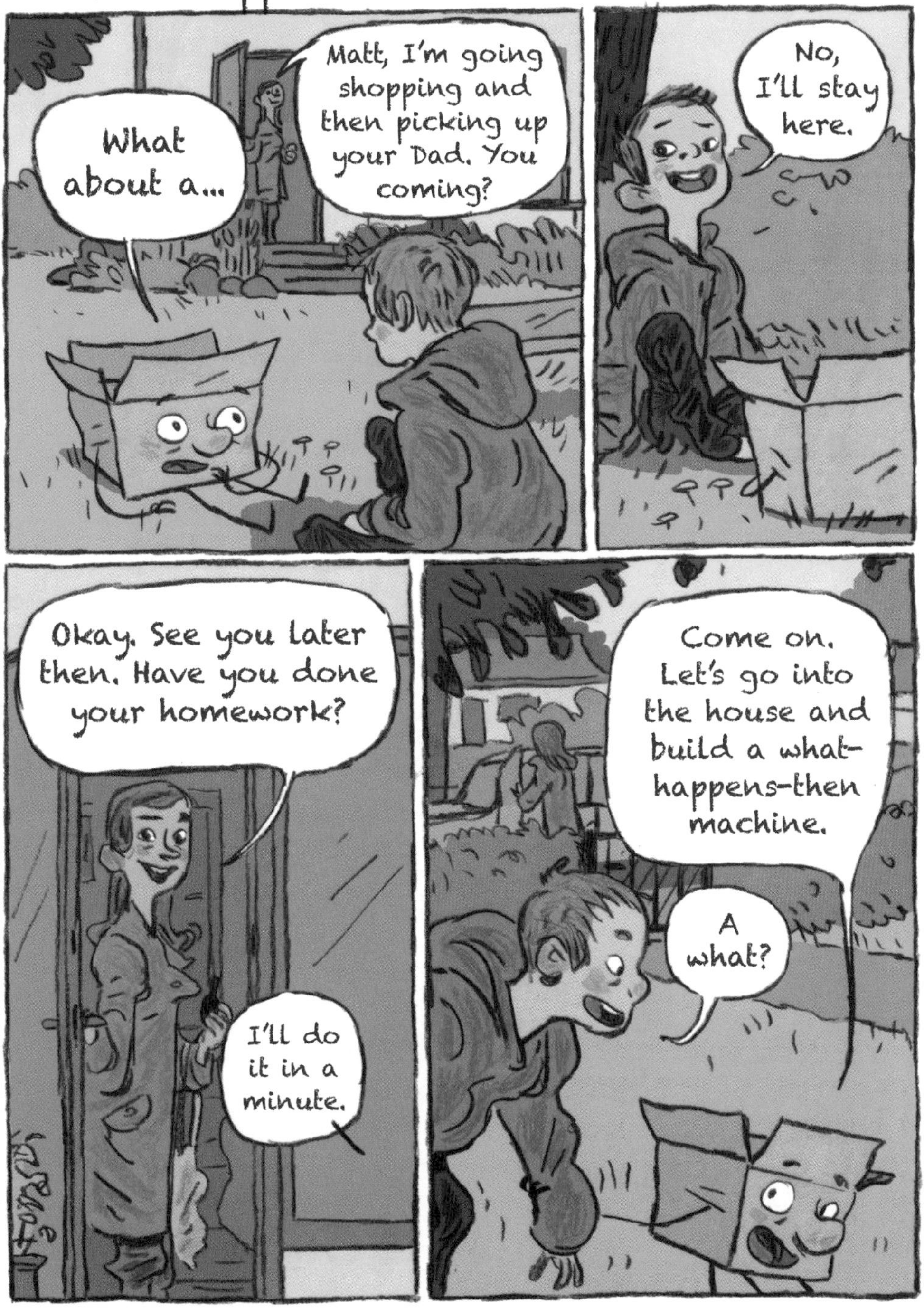

What about a...
Matt, I'm going shopping and then picking up your Dad. You coming?
No, I'll stay here.
Okay. See you later then. Have you done your homework?
I'll do it in a minute.
Come on. Let's go into the house and build a what-happens-then machine.
A what?

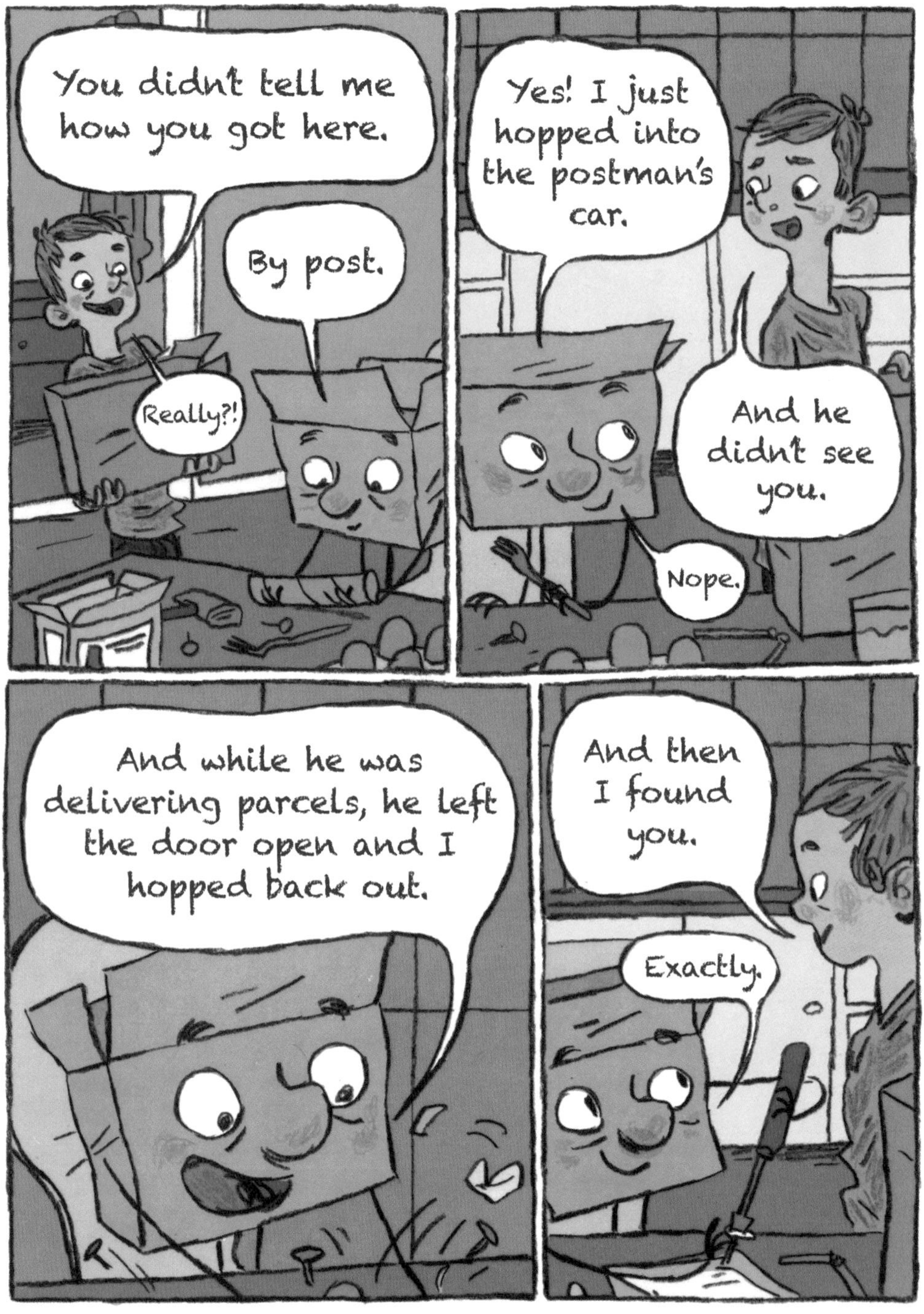
You didn't tell me how you got here.
By post.
Really?!
Yes! I just hopped into the postman's car.
And he didn't see you.
Nope.
And while he was delivering parcels, he left the door open and I hopped back out.
And then I found you.
Exactly.

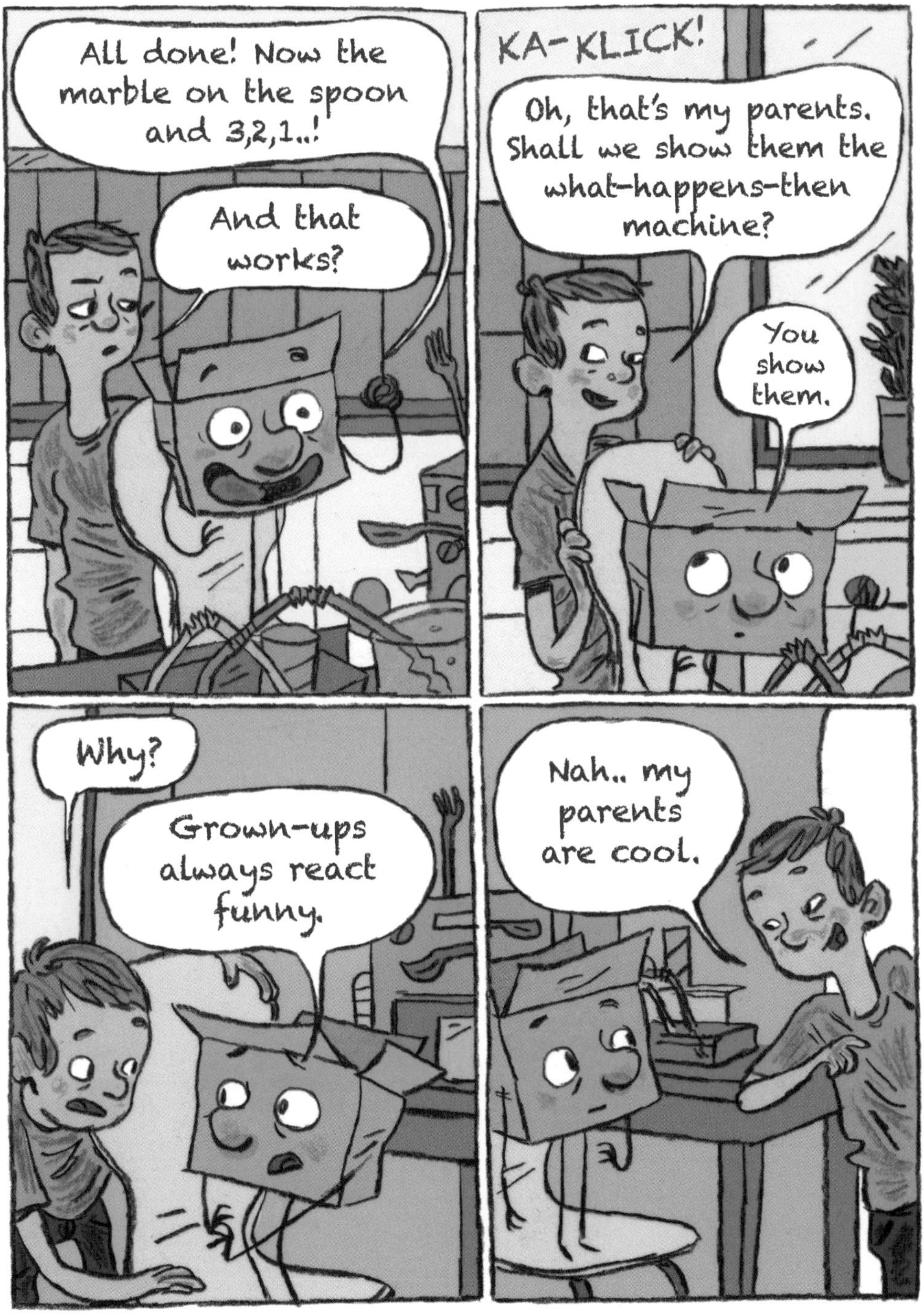
All done! Now the marble on the spoon and 3,2,1..!
And that works?
KA-KLICK!
Oh, that's my parents. Shall we show them the what-happens-then machine?
You show them.
Why?
Grown-ups always react funny.
Nah.. my parents are cool.

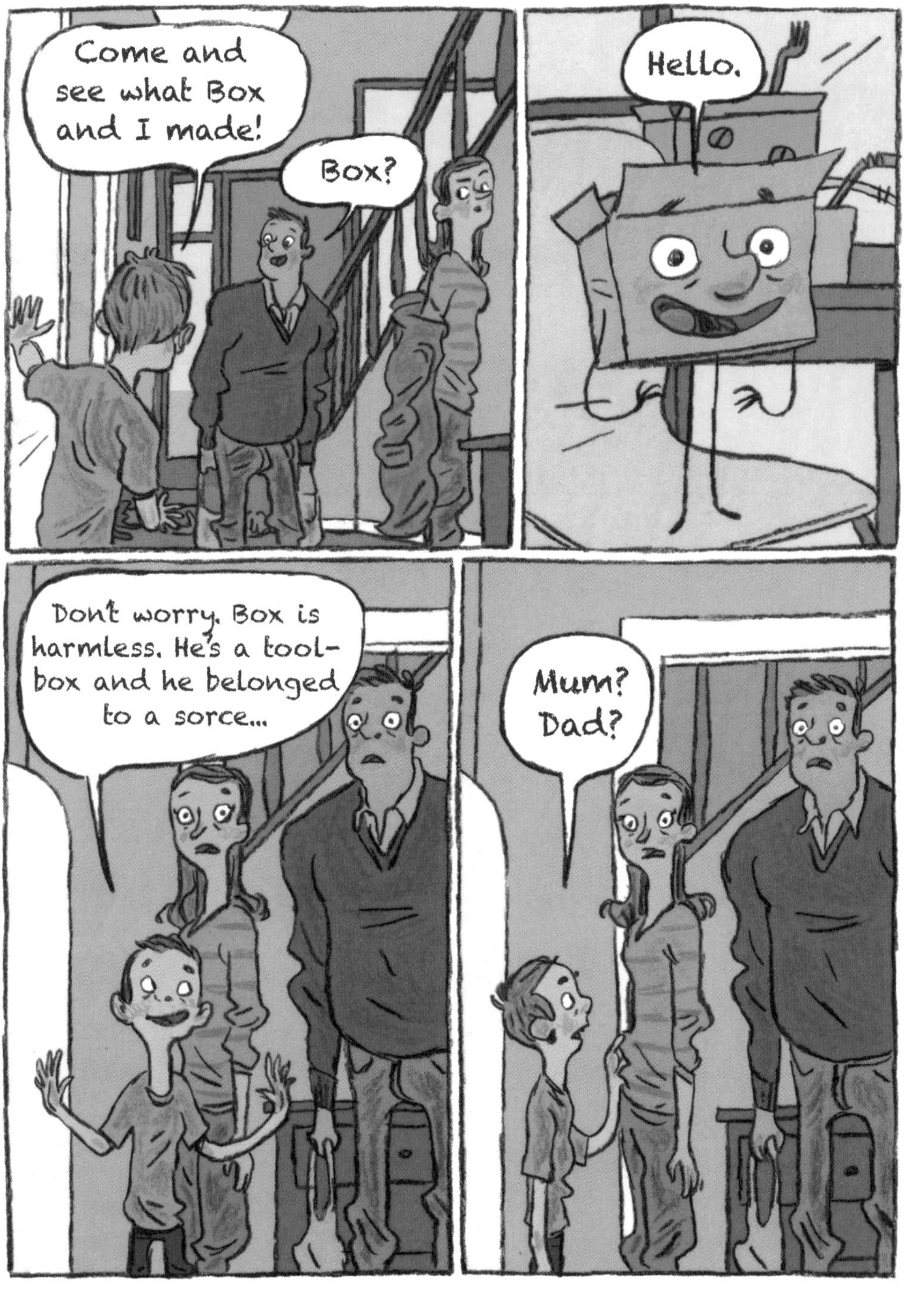
Come and see what Box and I made!
Box?
Hello.
Don't worry. Box is harmless. He's a tool-box and he belonged to a sorce...
Mum? Dad?

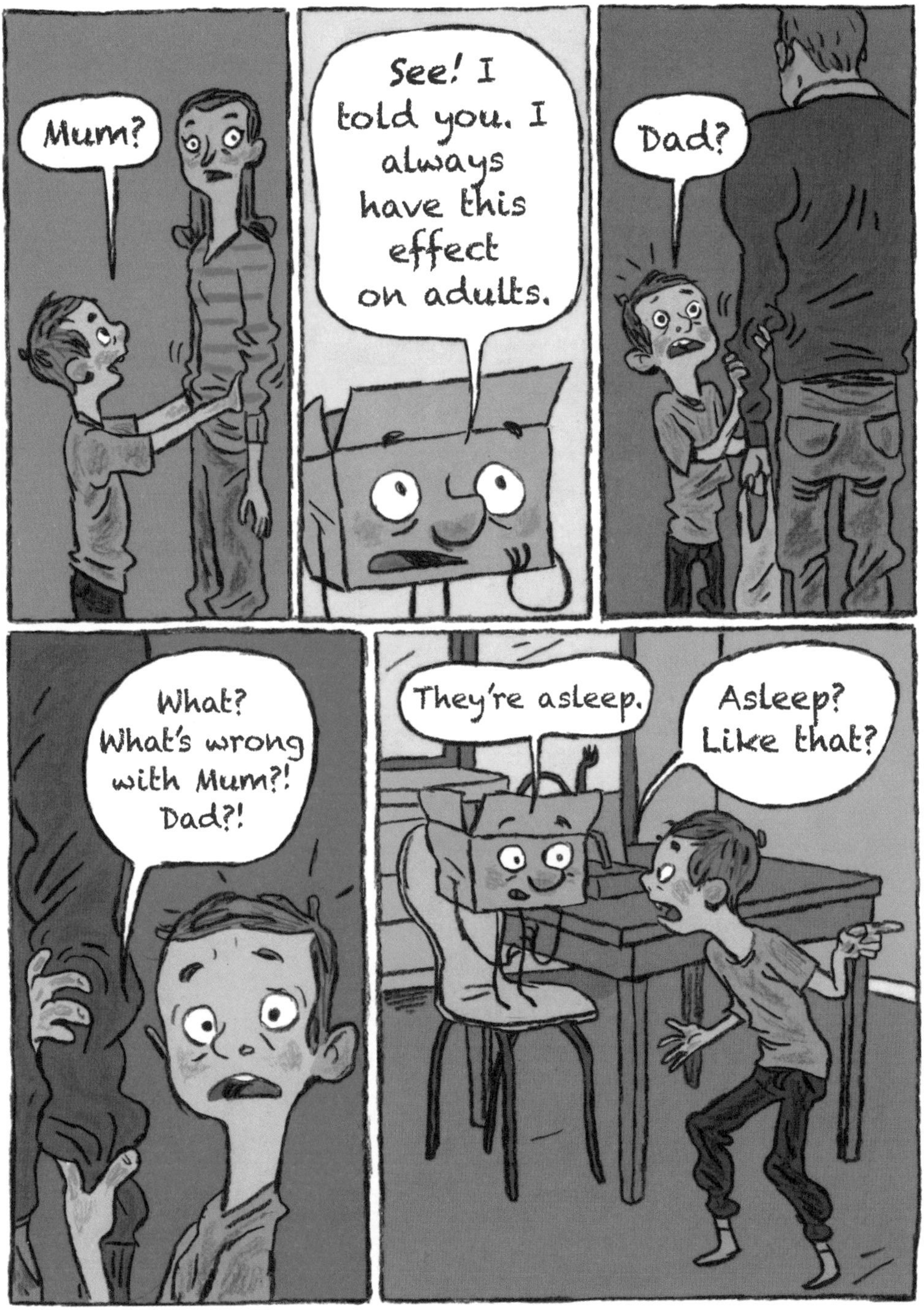
Mum?
See! I told you. I always have this effect on adults.
Dad?
What? What's wrong with Mum?! Dad?!
They're asleep.
Asleep? Like that?

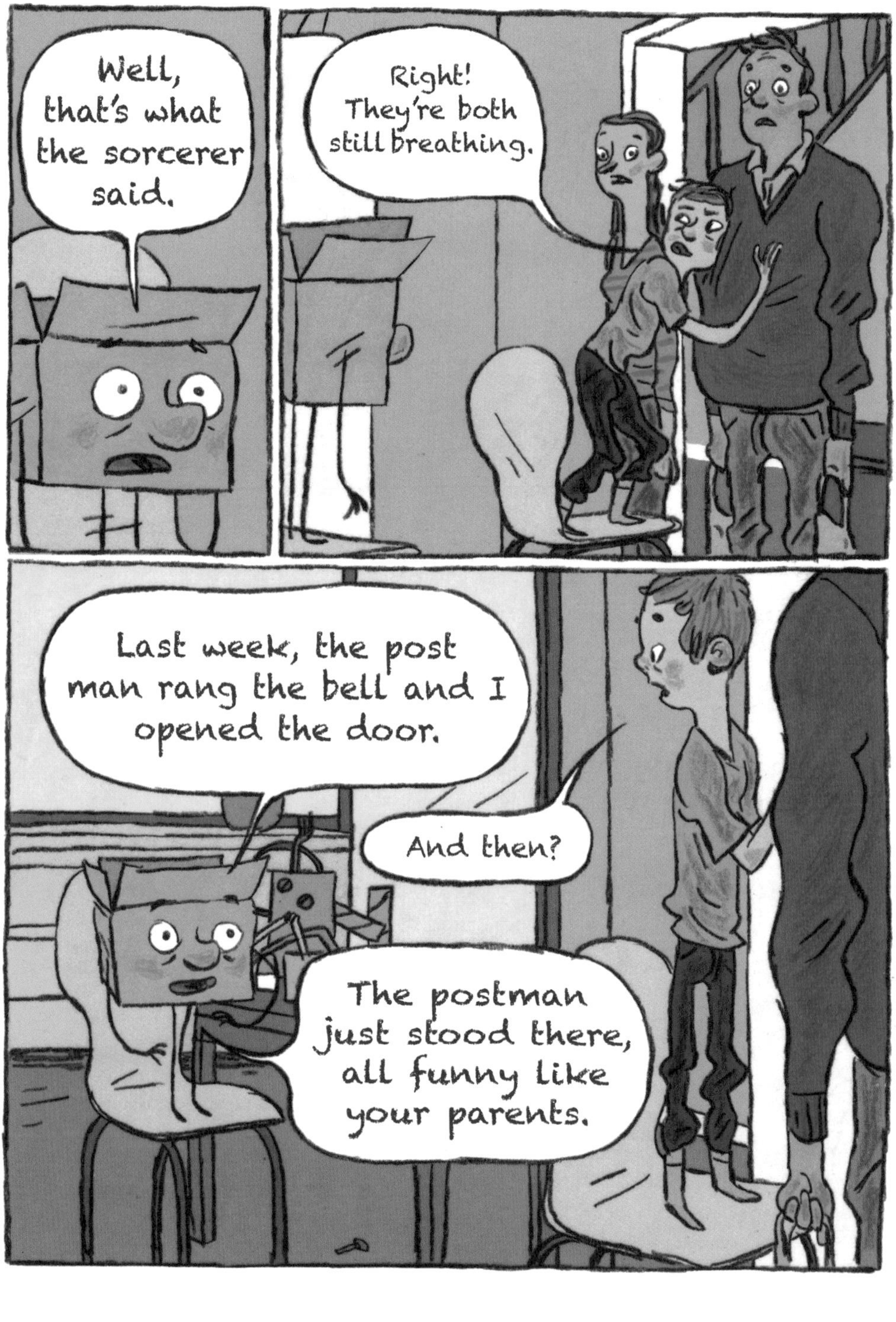
Well, that's what the sorcerer said.
Right! They're both still breathing.
Last week, the post man rang the bell and I opened the door.
And then?
The postman just stood there, all funny like your parents.

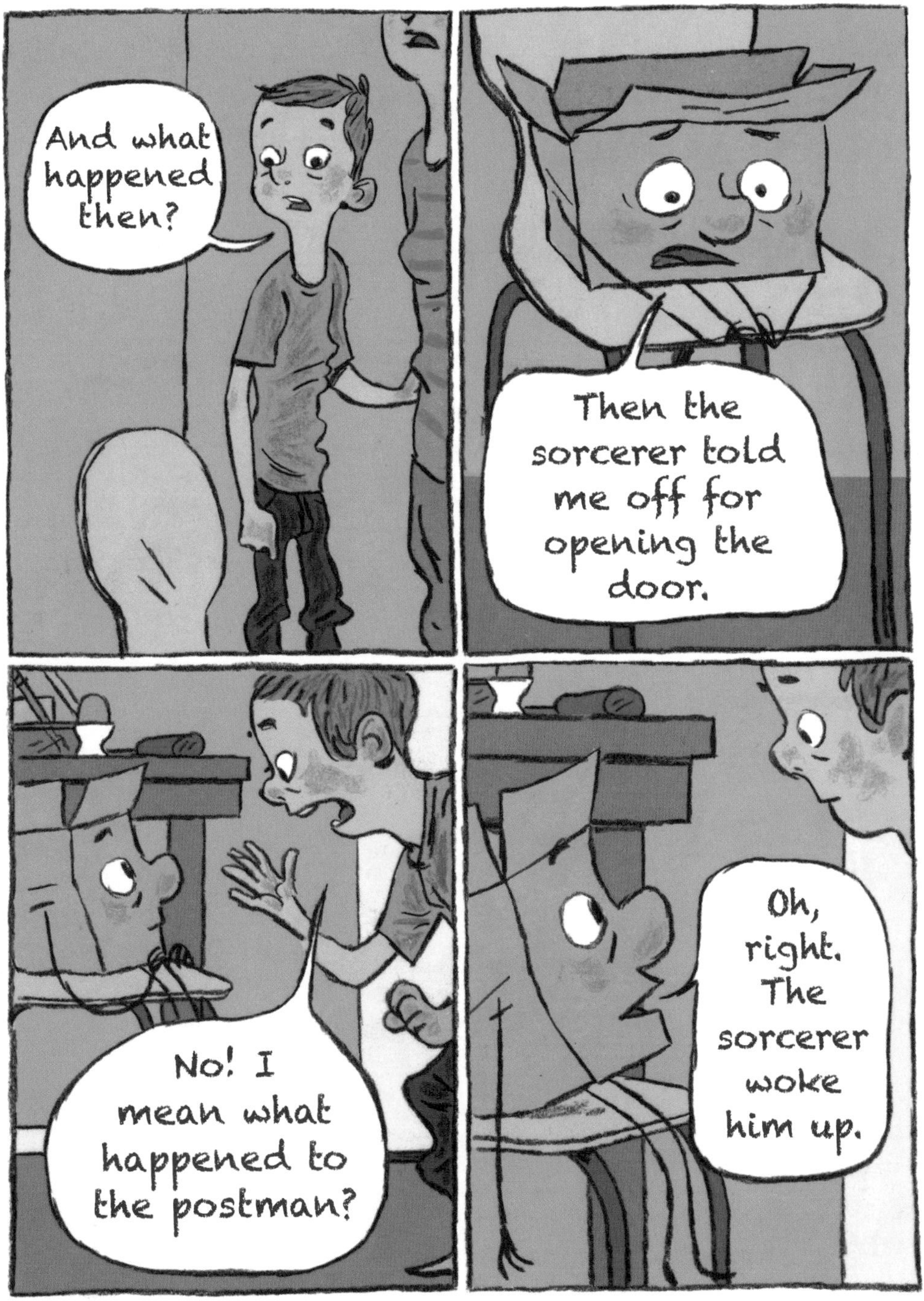
And what happened then?
Then the sorcerer told me off for opening the door.
No! I mean what happened to the postman?
Oh, right. The sorcerer woke him up.

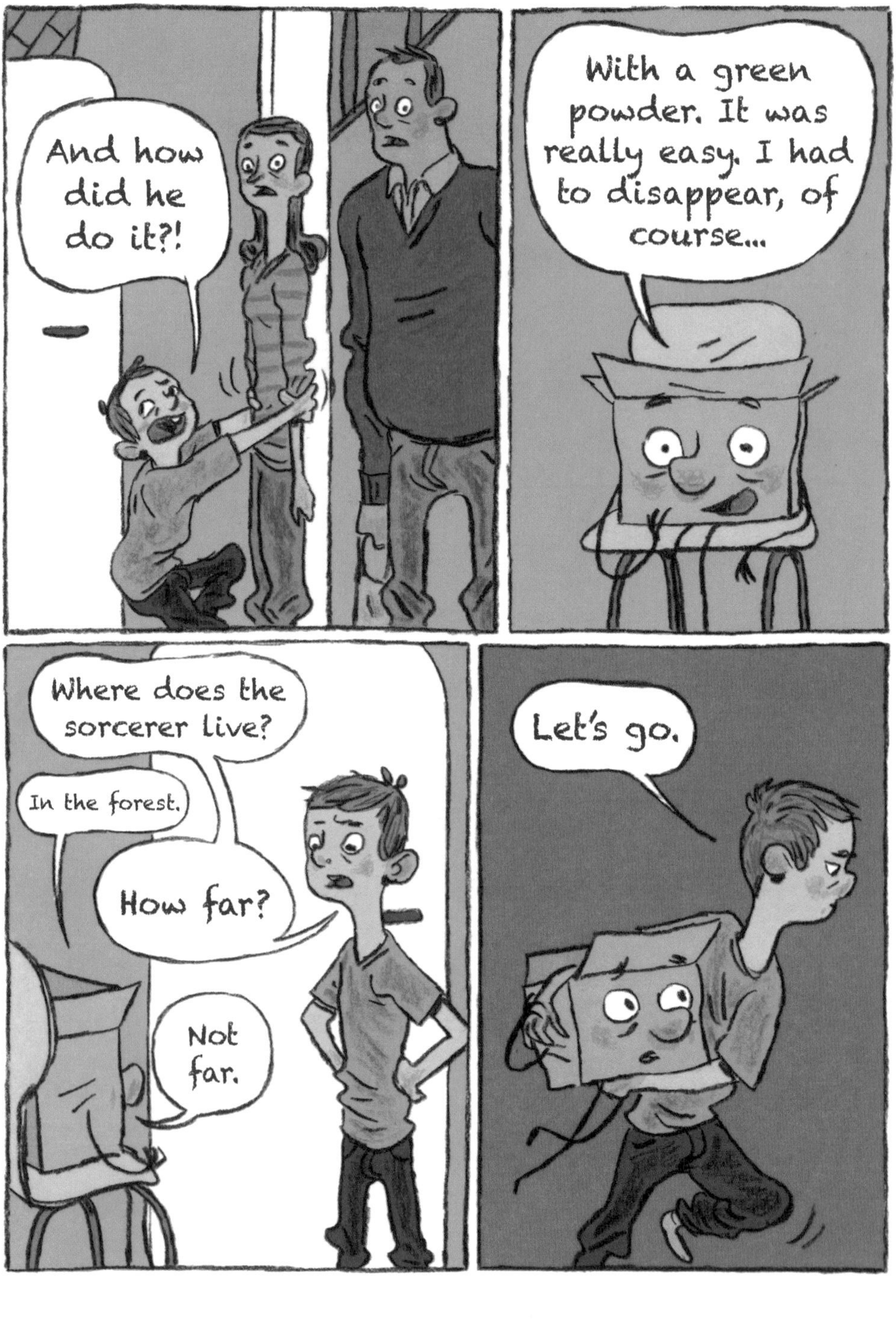
And how did he do it?!
With a green powder. It was really easy. I had to disappear, of course...
Where does the sorcerer live?
In the forest.
How far?
Not far.
Let's go.

The House in the Forest

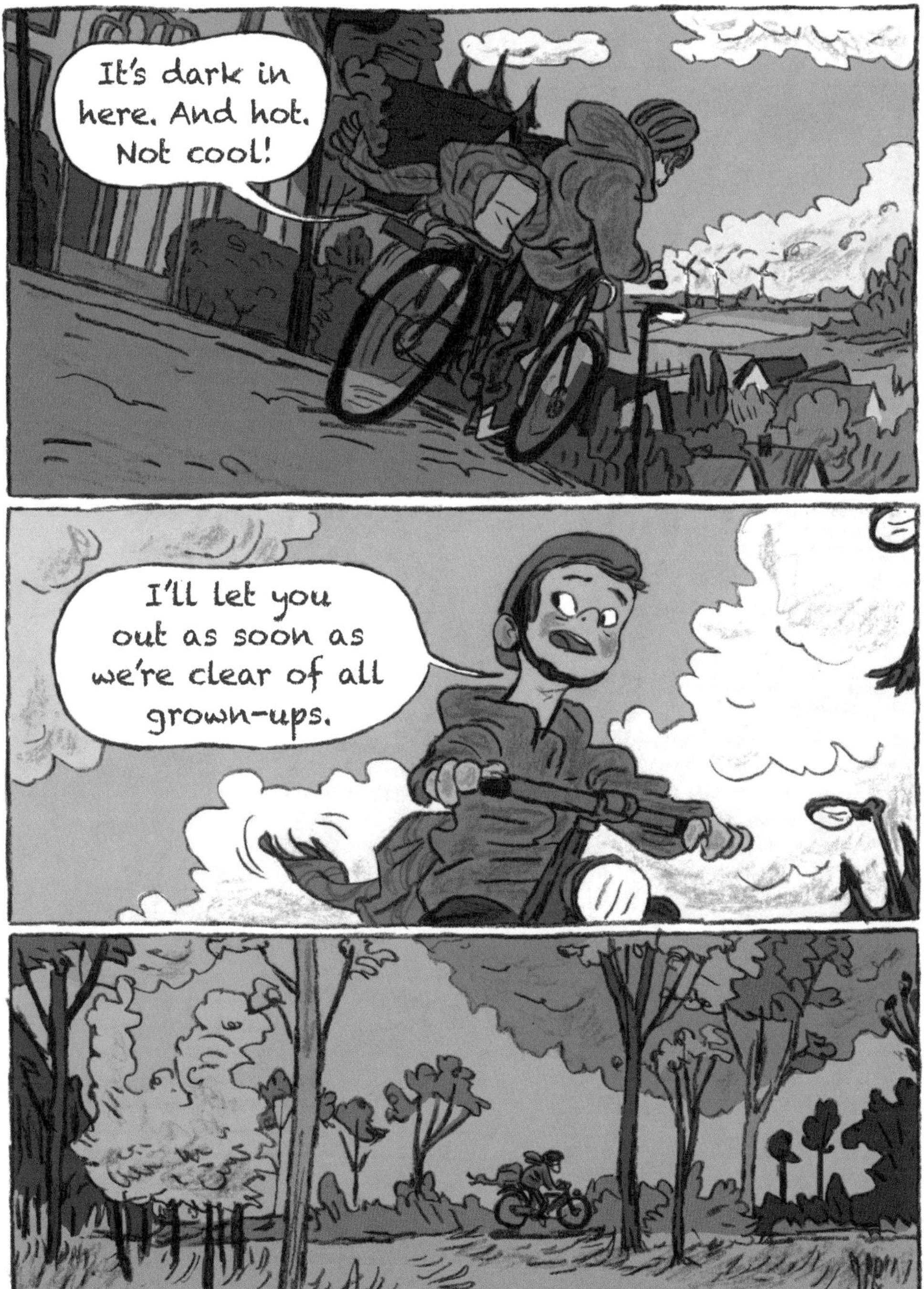
It's dark in here. And hot. Not cool!
I'll let you out as soon as we're clear of all grown-ups.

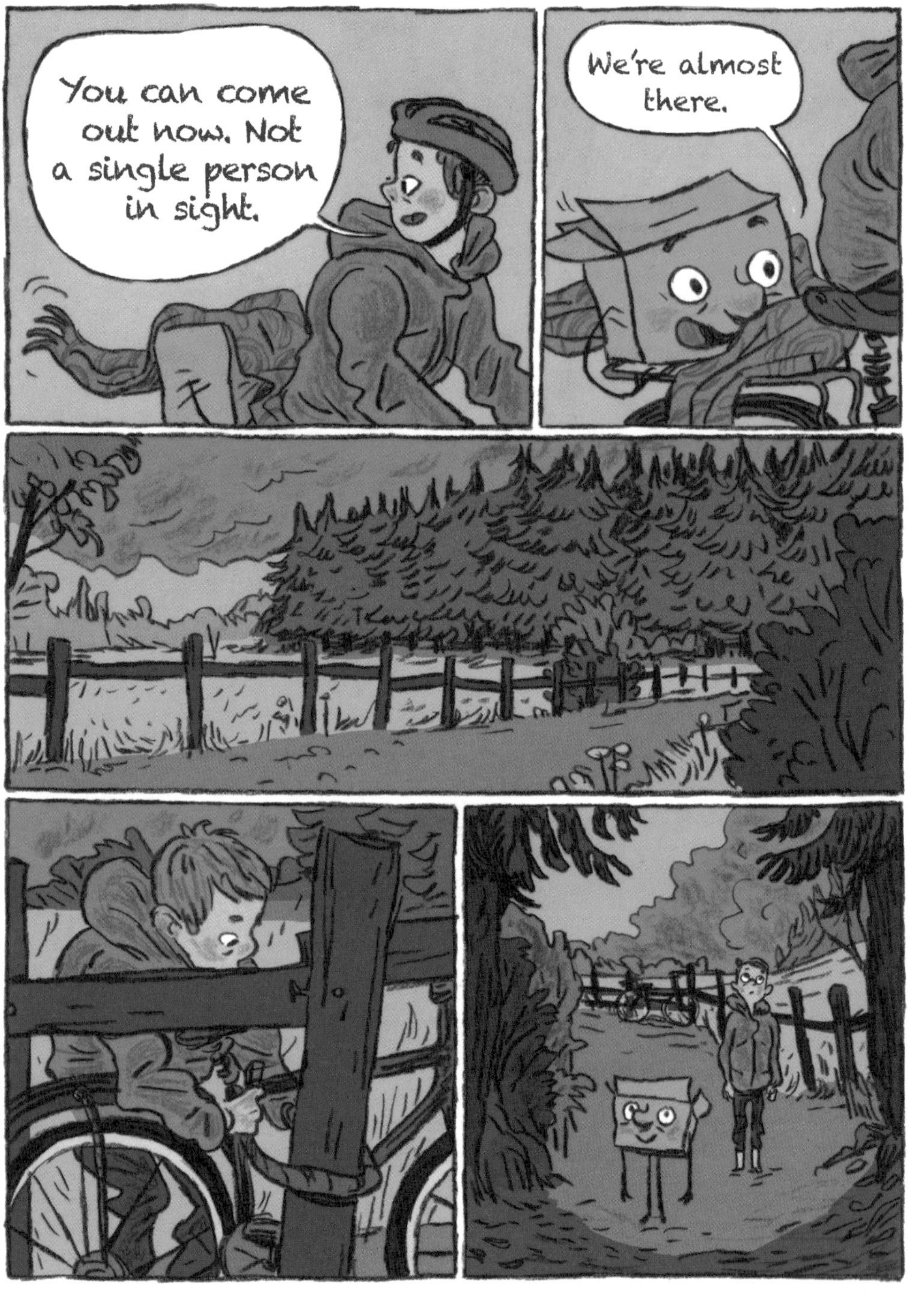
You can come out now. Not a single person in sight.
We're almost there.

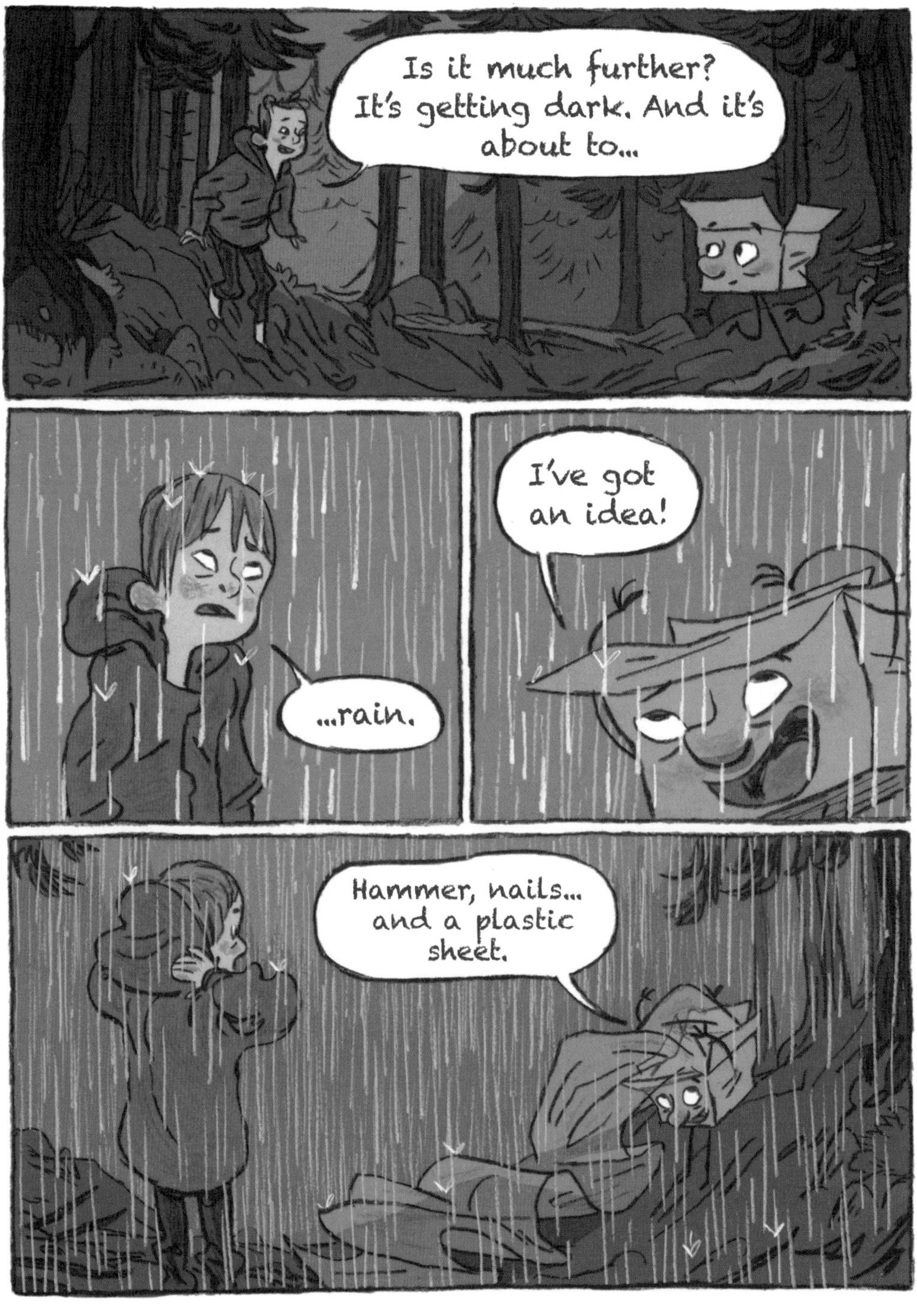
Is it much further? It's getting dark. And it's about to...
...rain.
I've got an idea!
Hammer, nails... and a plastic sheet.

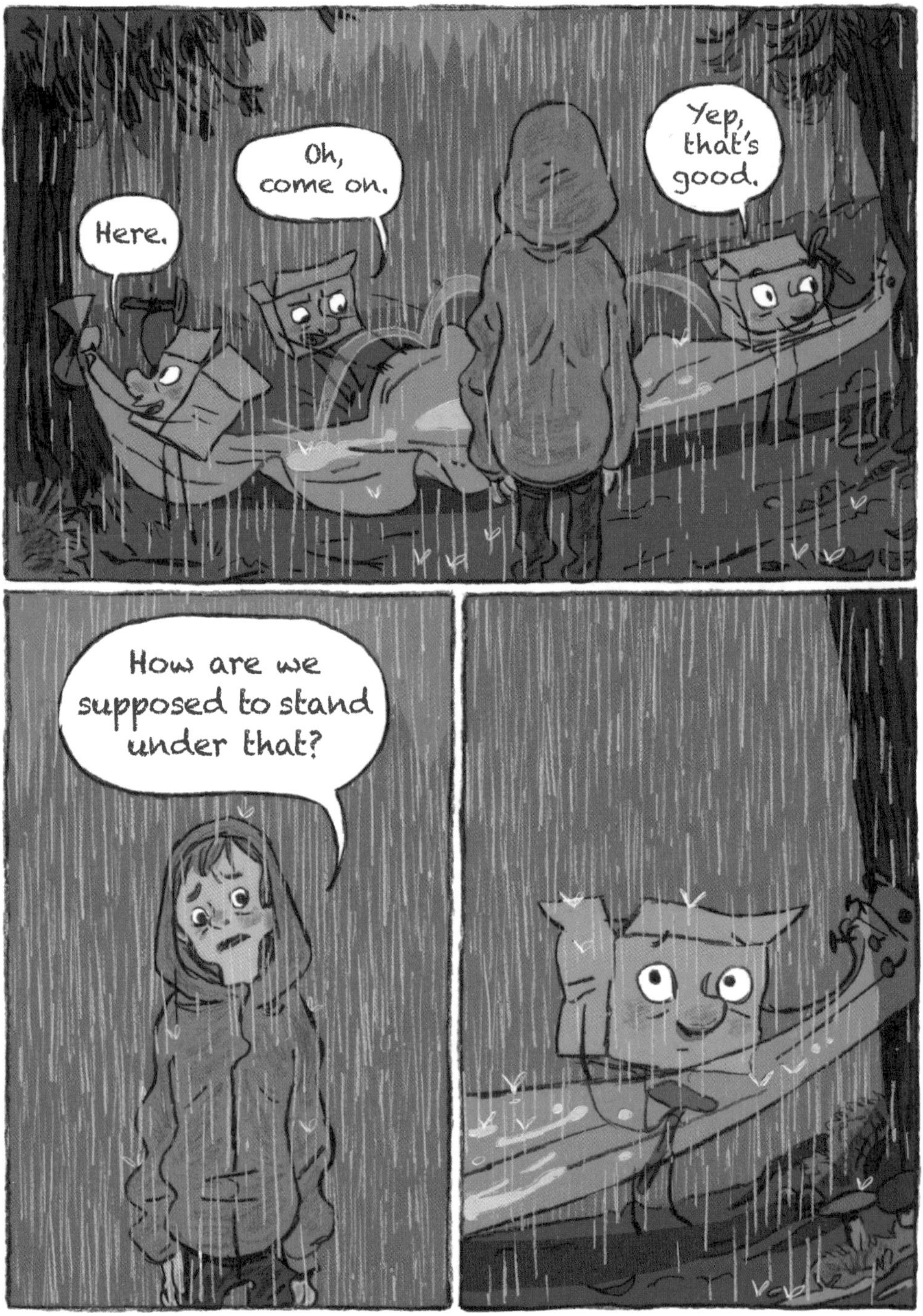
Here.
Oh, come on.
Yep, that's good.
How are we supposed to stand under that?

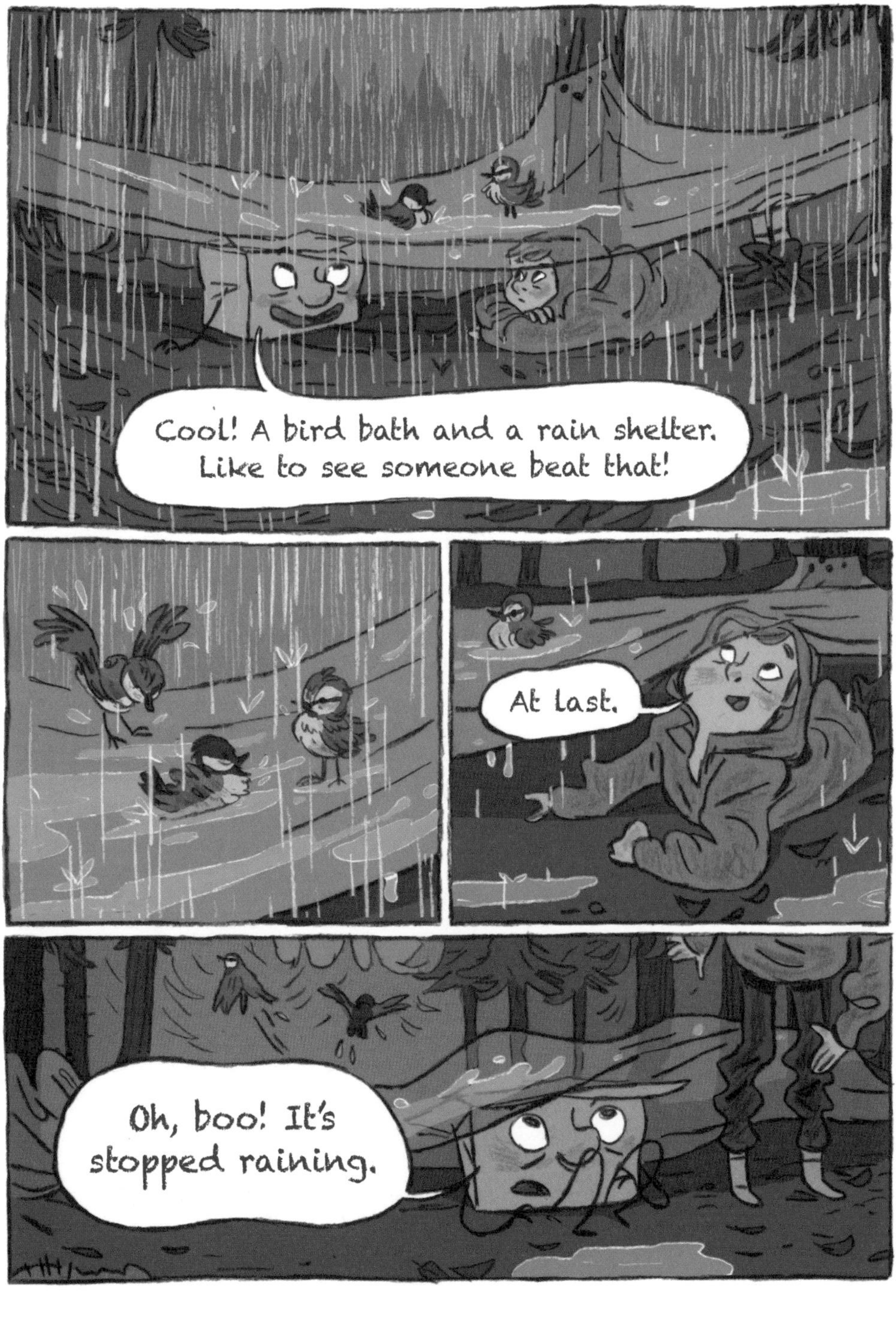
Cool! A bird bath and a rain shelter. Like to see someone beat that!
At last.
Oh, boo! It's stopped raining.

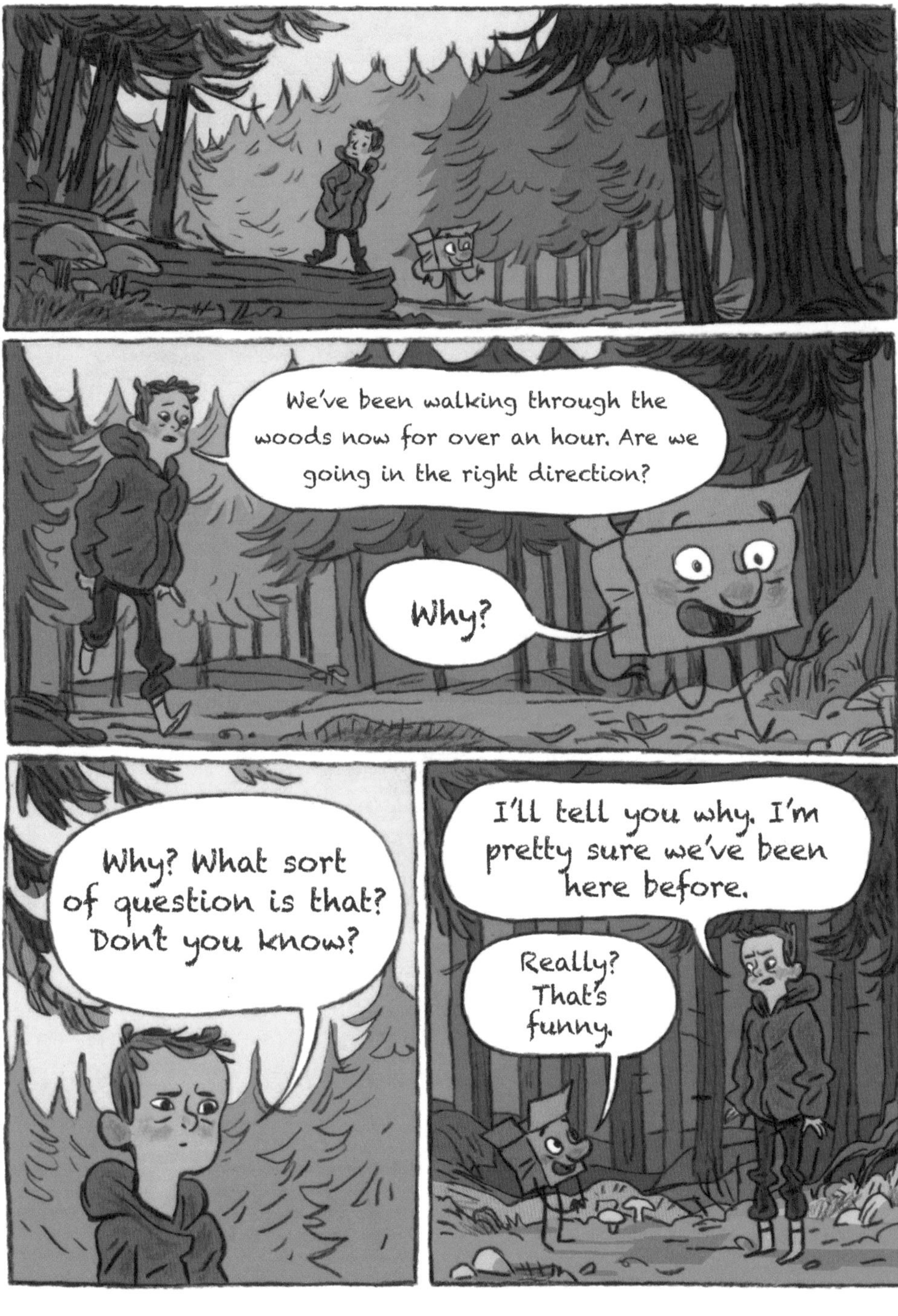

We've been walking through the woods now for over an hour. Are we going in the right direction?
Why?
Why? What sort of question is that? Don't you know?
I'll tell you why. I'm pretty sure we've been here before.
Really? That's funny.

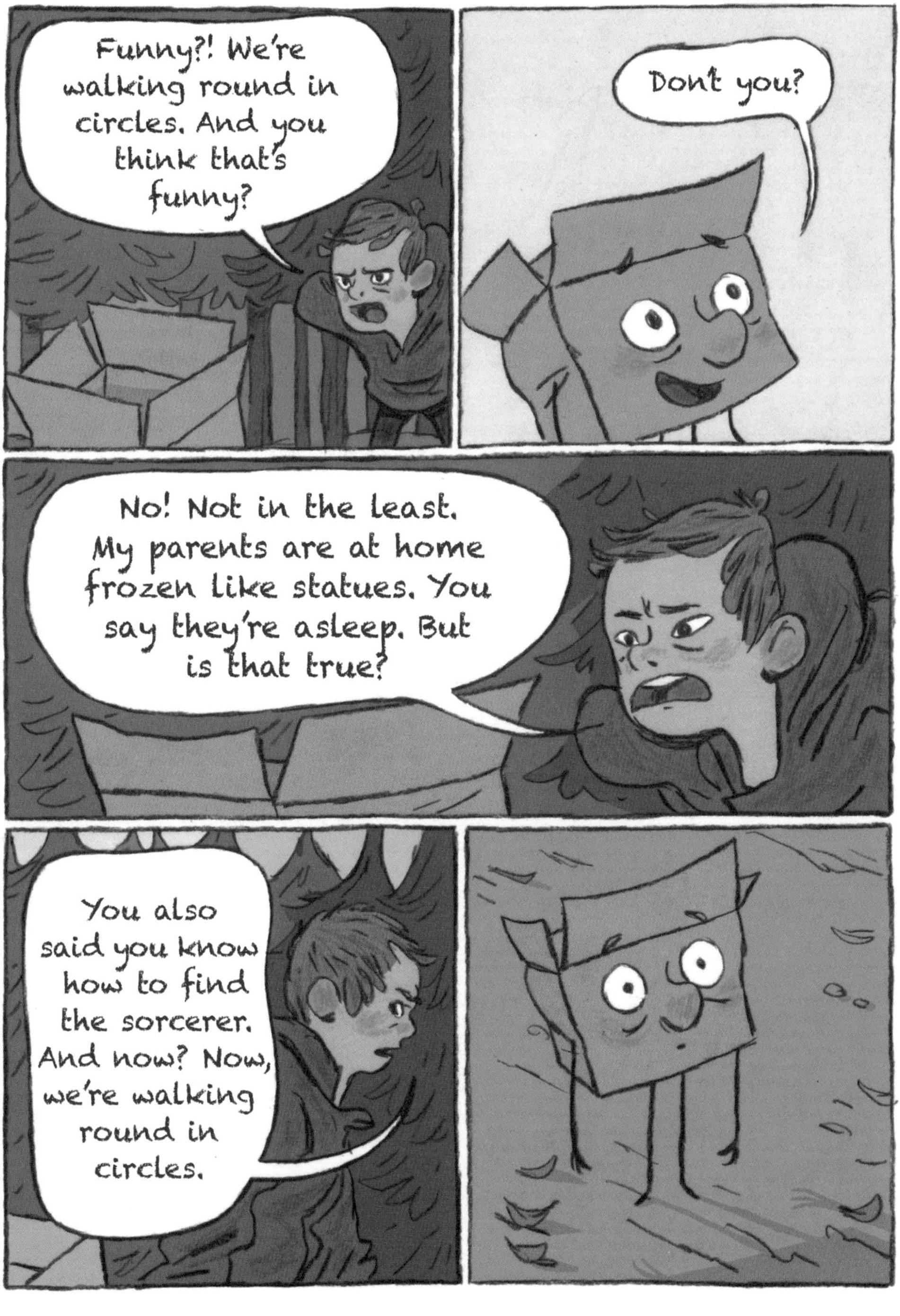
Funny?! We're walking round in circles. And you think that's funny?
Don't you?
No! Not in the least. My parents are at home frozen like statues. You say they're asleep. But is that true?
You also said you know how to find the sorcerer. And now? Now, we're walking round in circles.

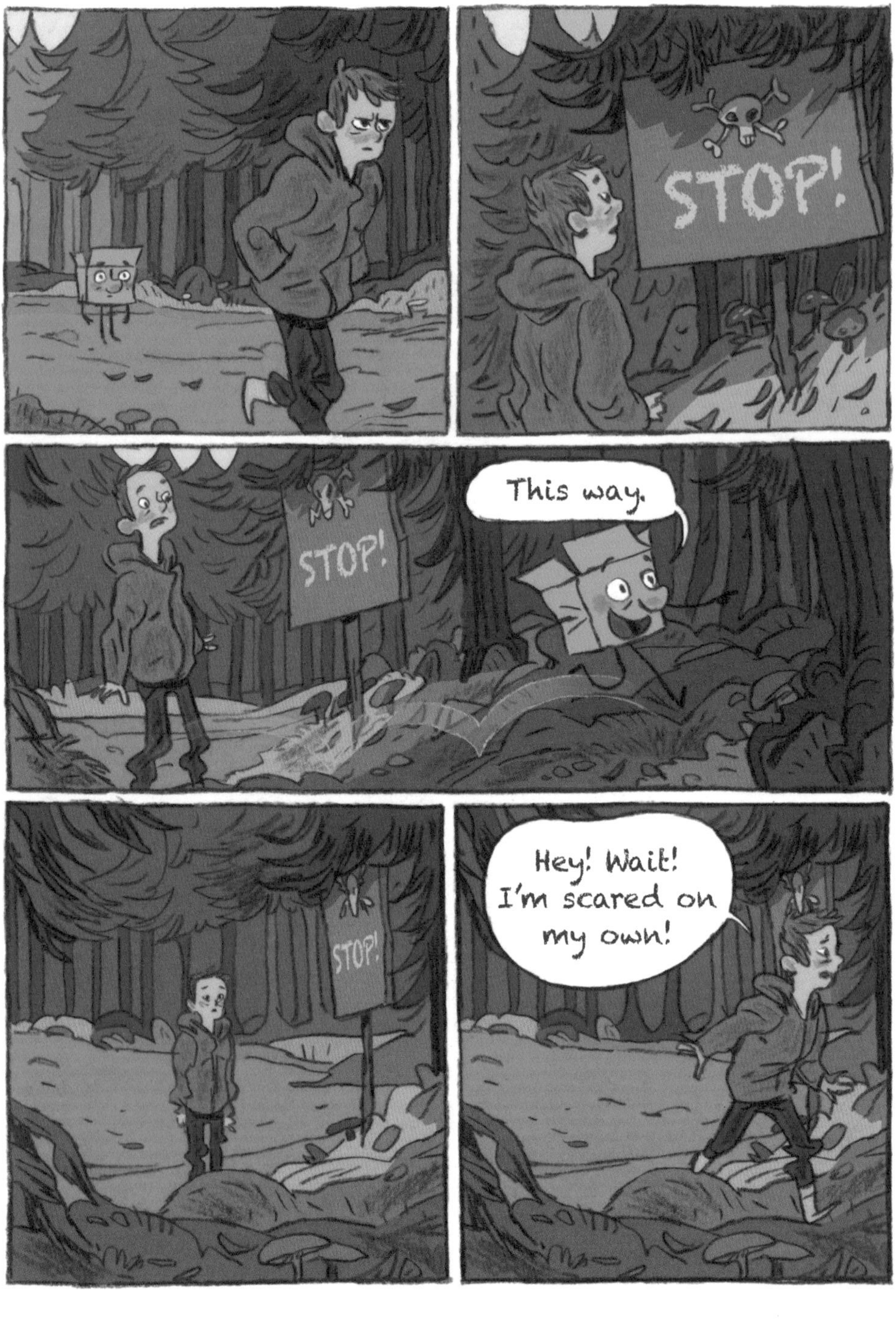
STOP!
STOP!
This way.
STOP!
Hey! Wait! I'm scared on my own!

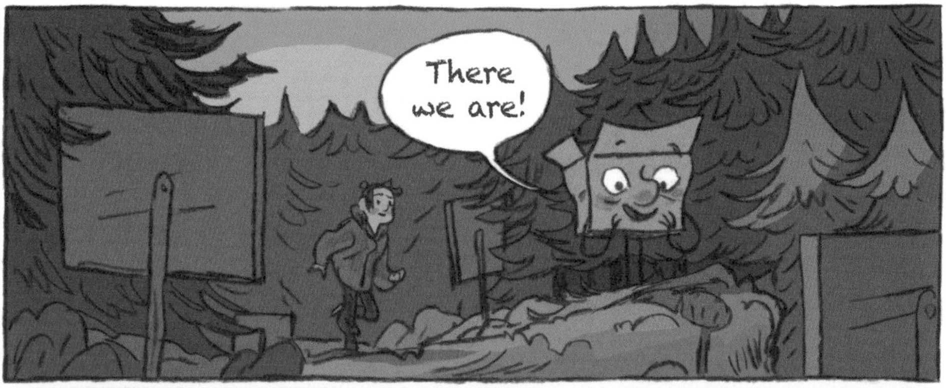
There we are!

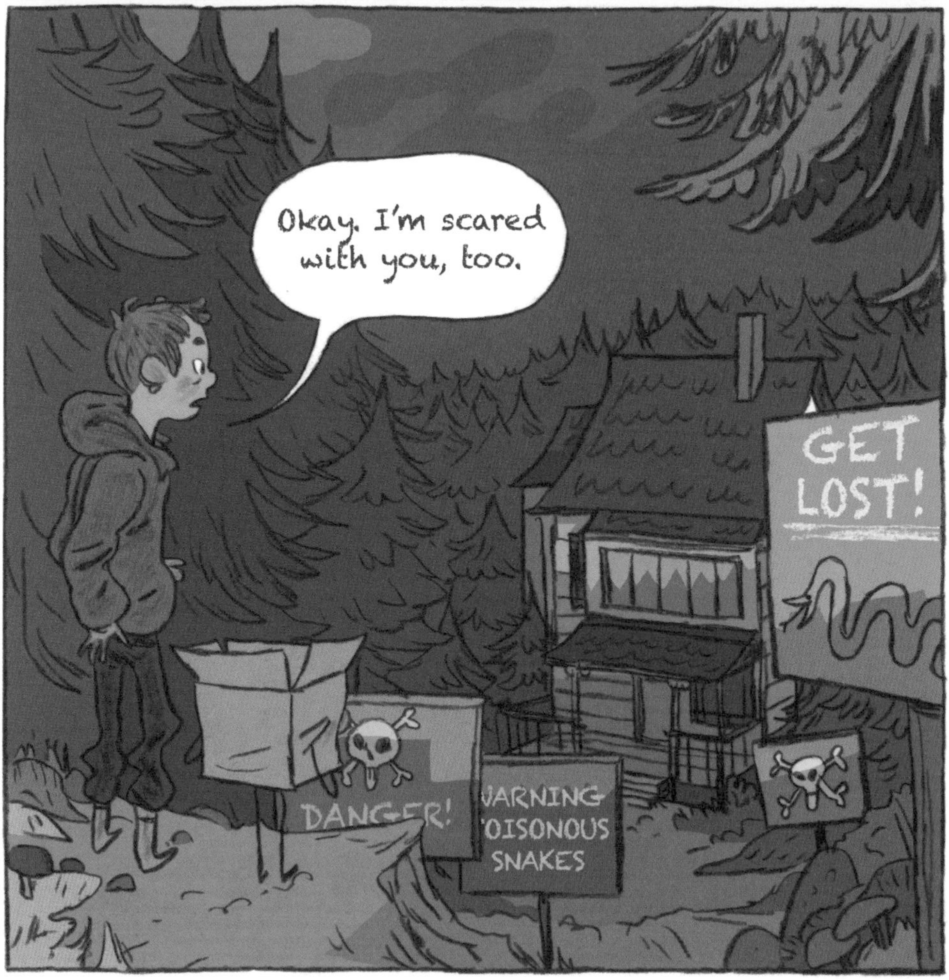
Okay. I'm scared with you, too.
GET LOST!
DANGER!
WARNING POISONOUS SNAKES

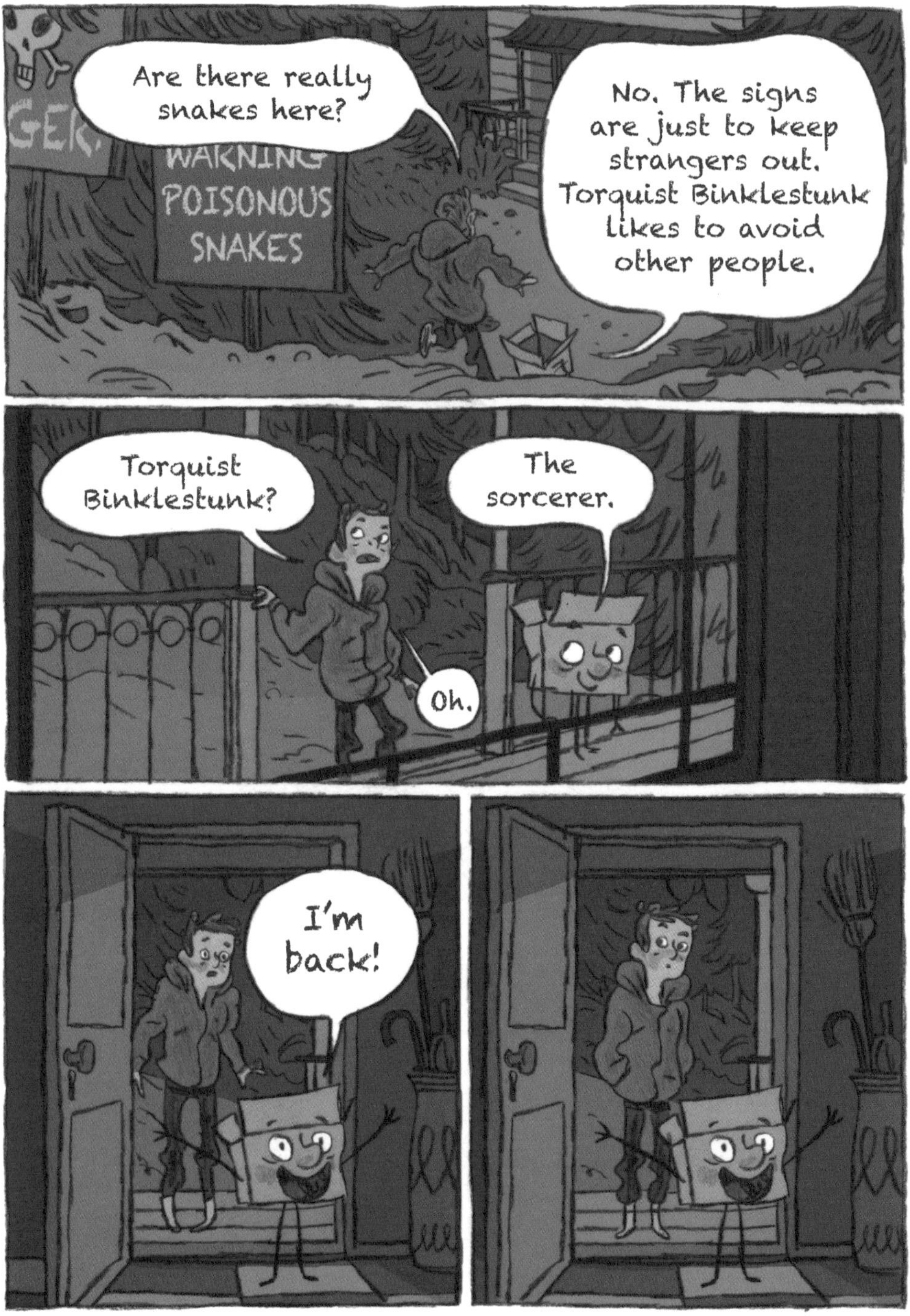

WARNING
POISONOUS
SNAKES
Are there really snakes here?
No. The signs are just to keep strangers out. Torquist Binklestunk likes to avoid other people.
Torquist Binklestunk?
The sorcerer.
Oh.
I'm back!

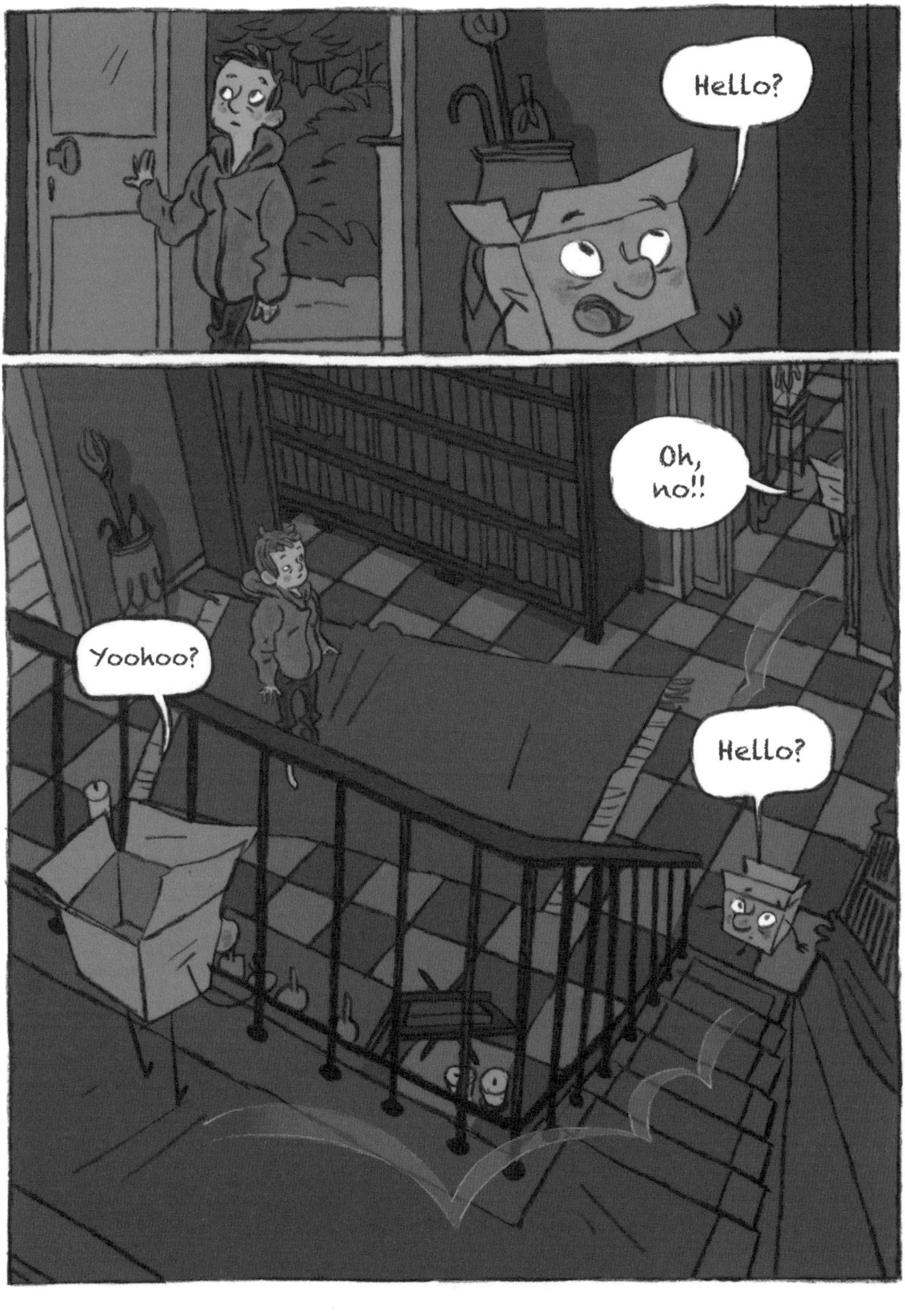
Hello?
Oh, no!!
Yoohoo?
Hello?

Torquist Binklestunk

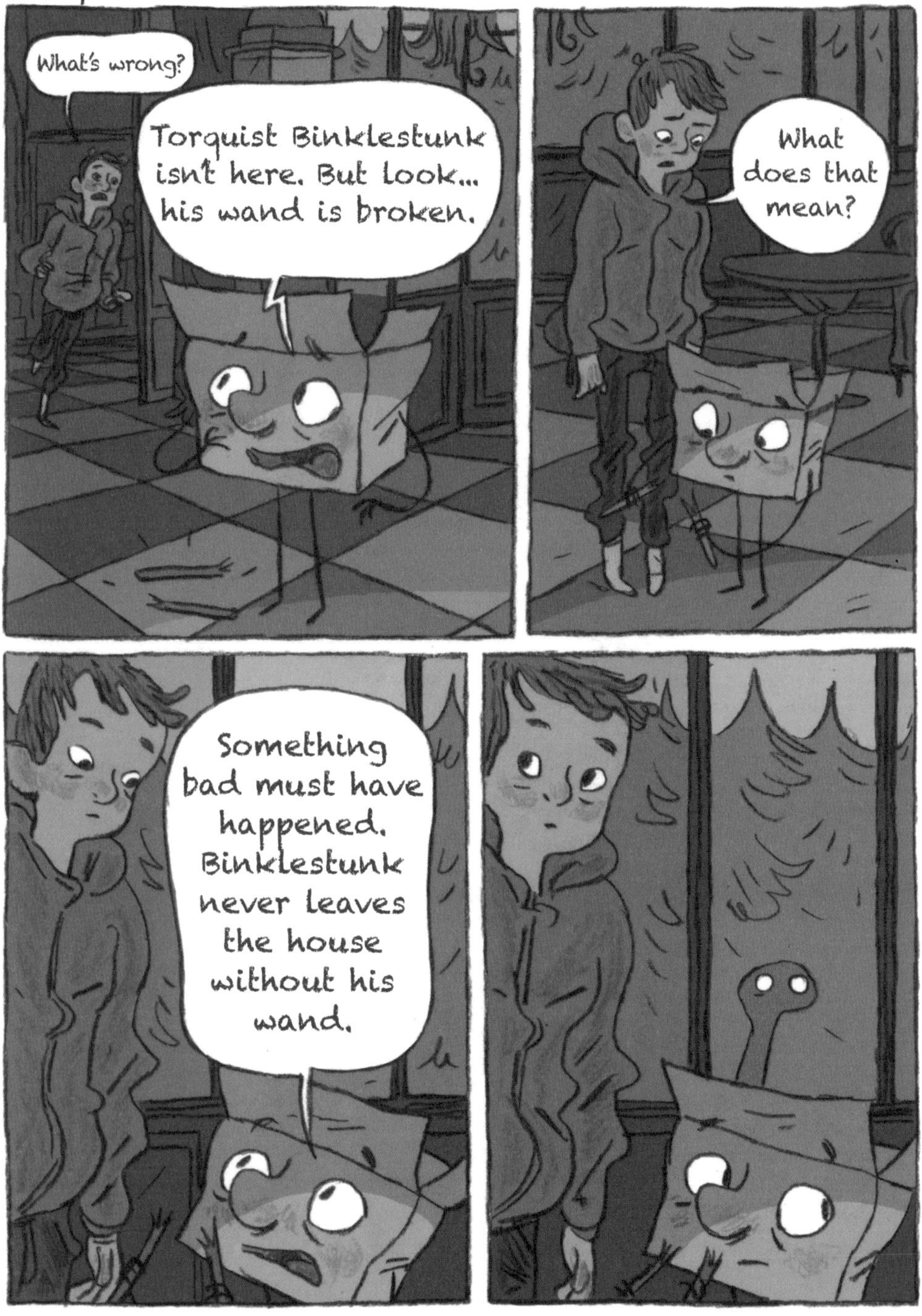
What's wrong?
Torquist Binklestunk isn't here. But look... his wand is broken.
What does that mean?
Something bad must have happened. Binklestunk never leaves the house without his wand.

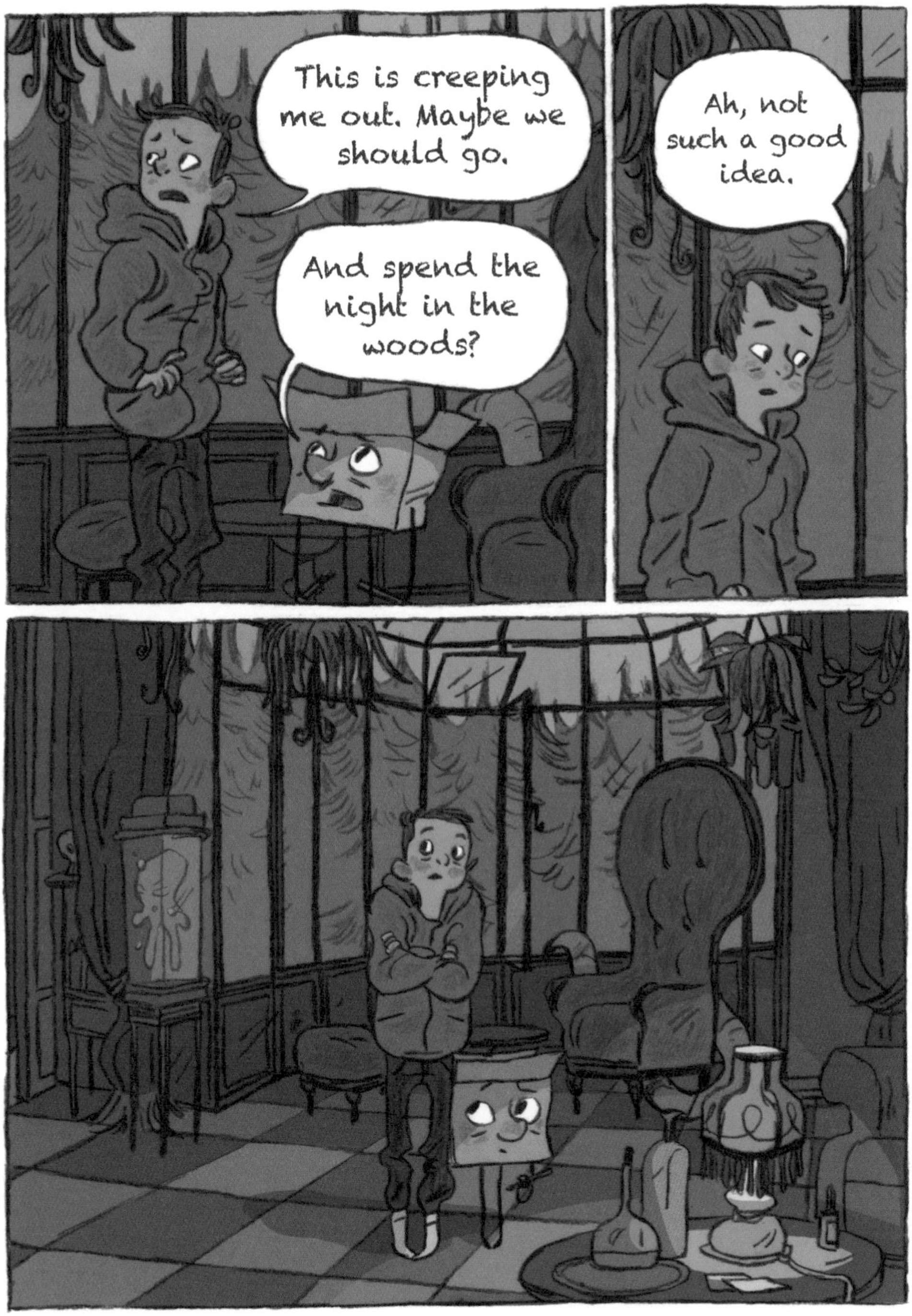
This is creeping me out. Maybe we should go.
And spend the night in the woods?
Ah, not such a good idea.

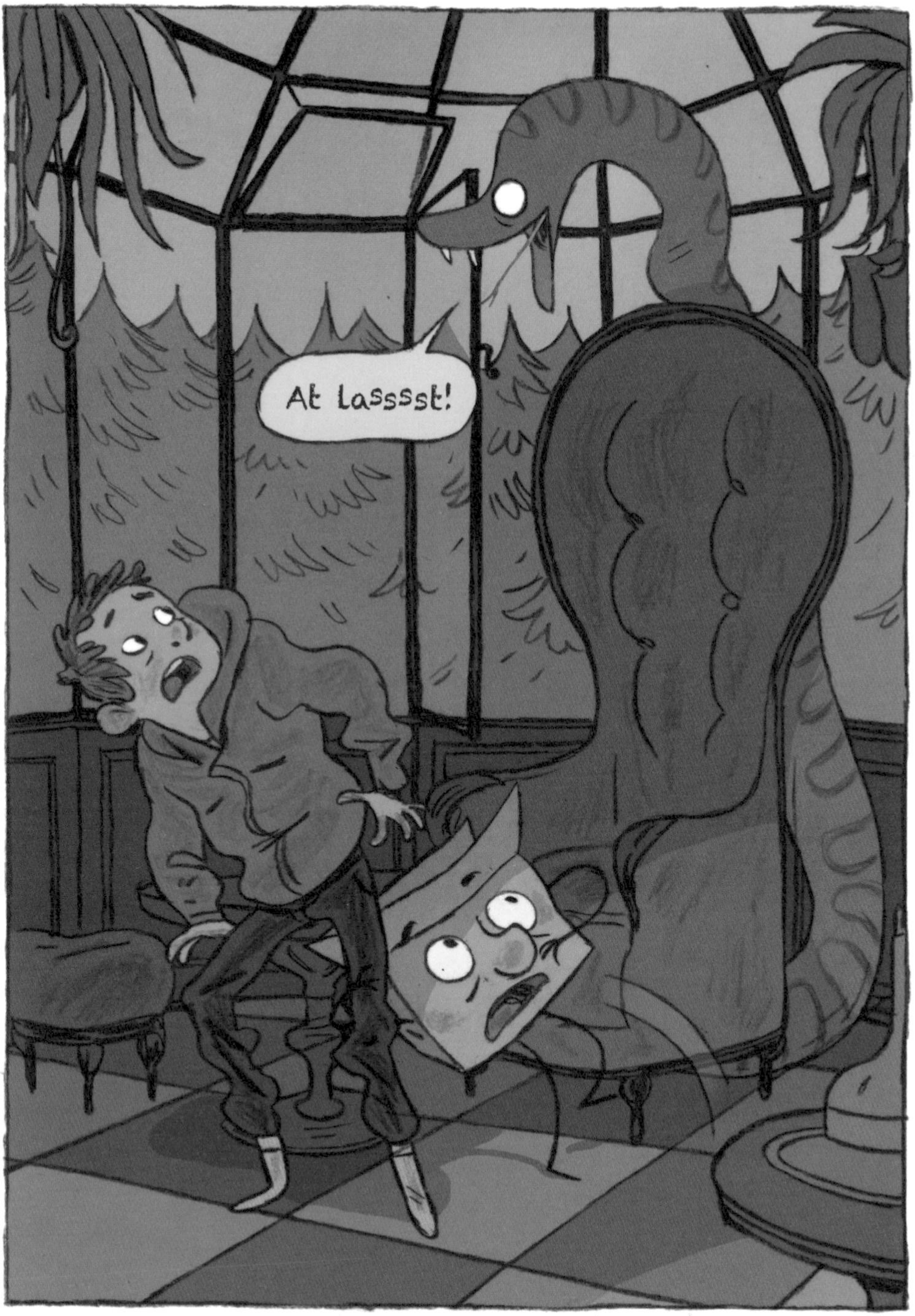
At lasssst!

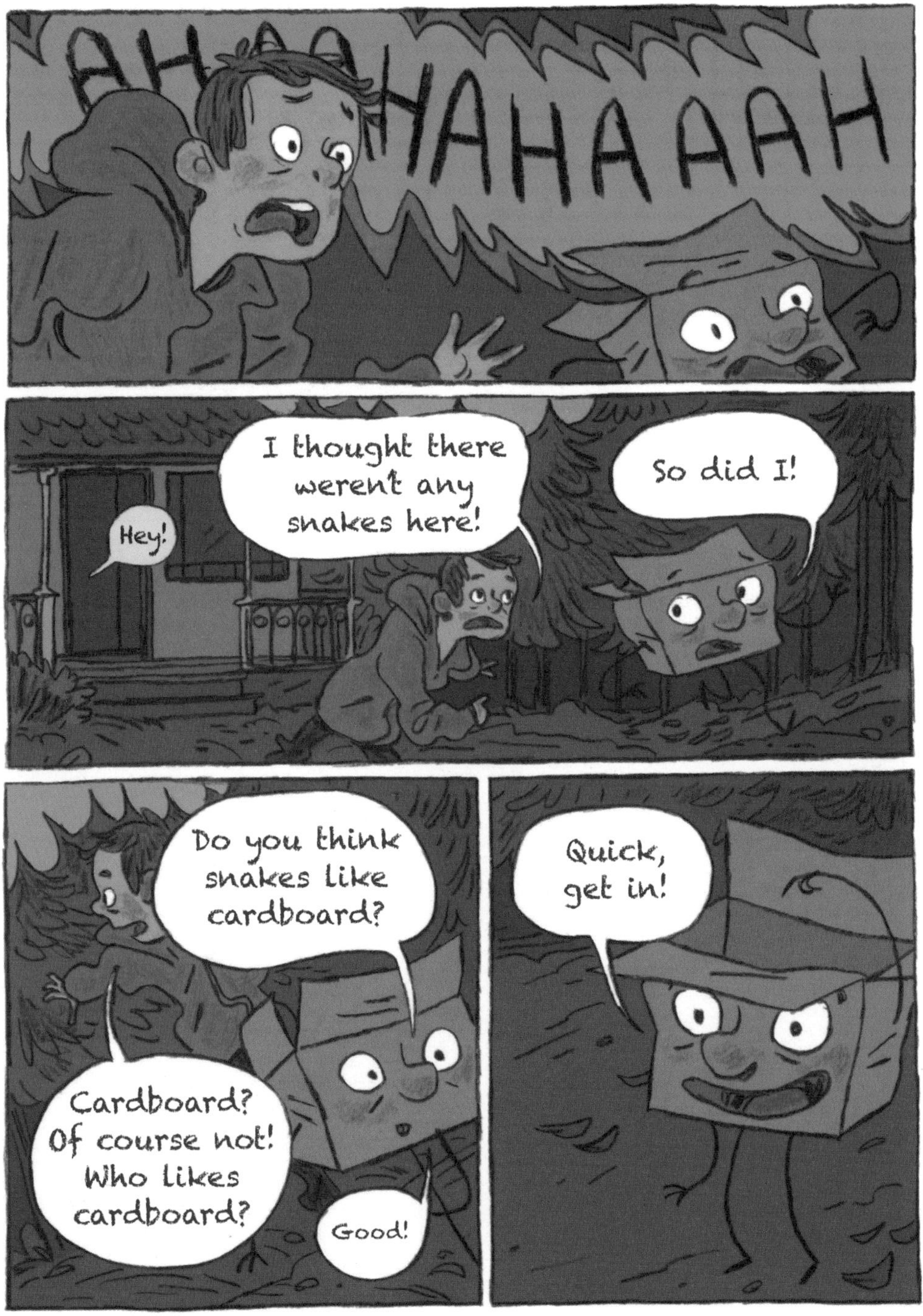
AHAAAHAHAAAH
Hey!
I thought there werent any snakes here!
So did I!
Do you think snakes like cardboard?
Cardboard? Of course not! Who likes cardboard?
Good!
Quick, get in!

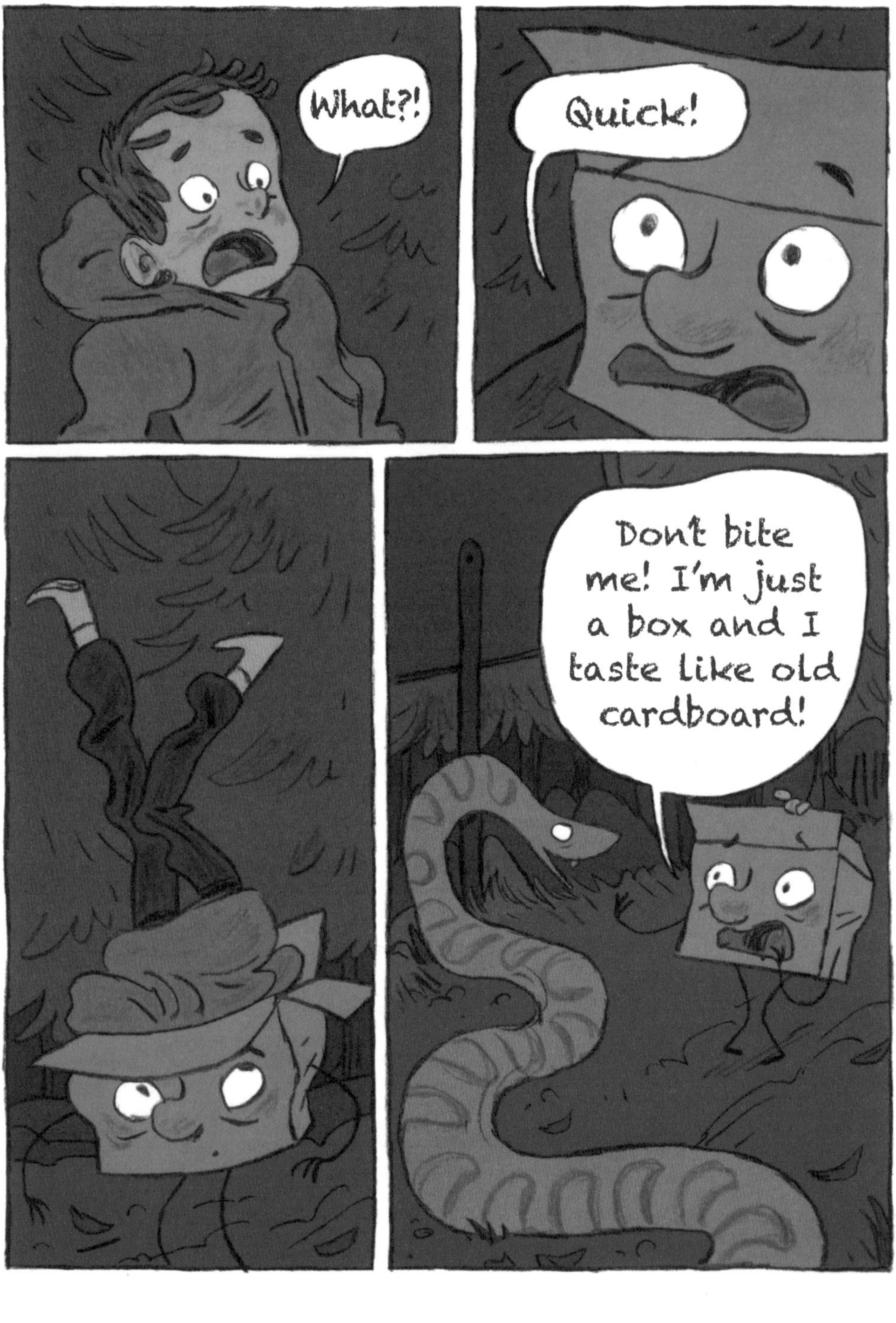
What?!
Quick!
Don't bite me! I'm just a box and I taste like old cardboard!

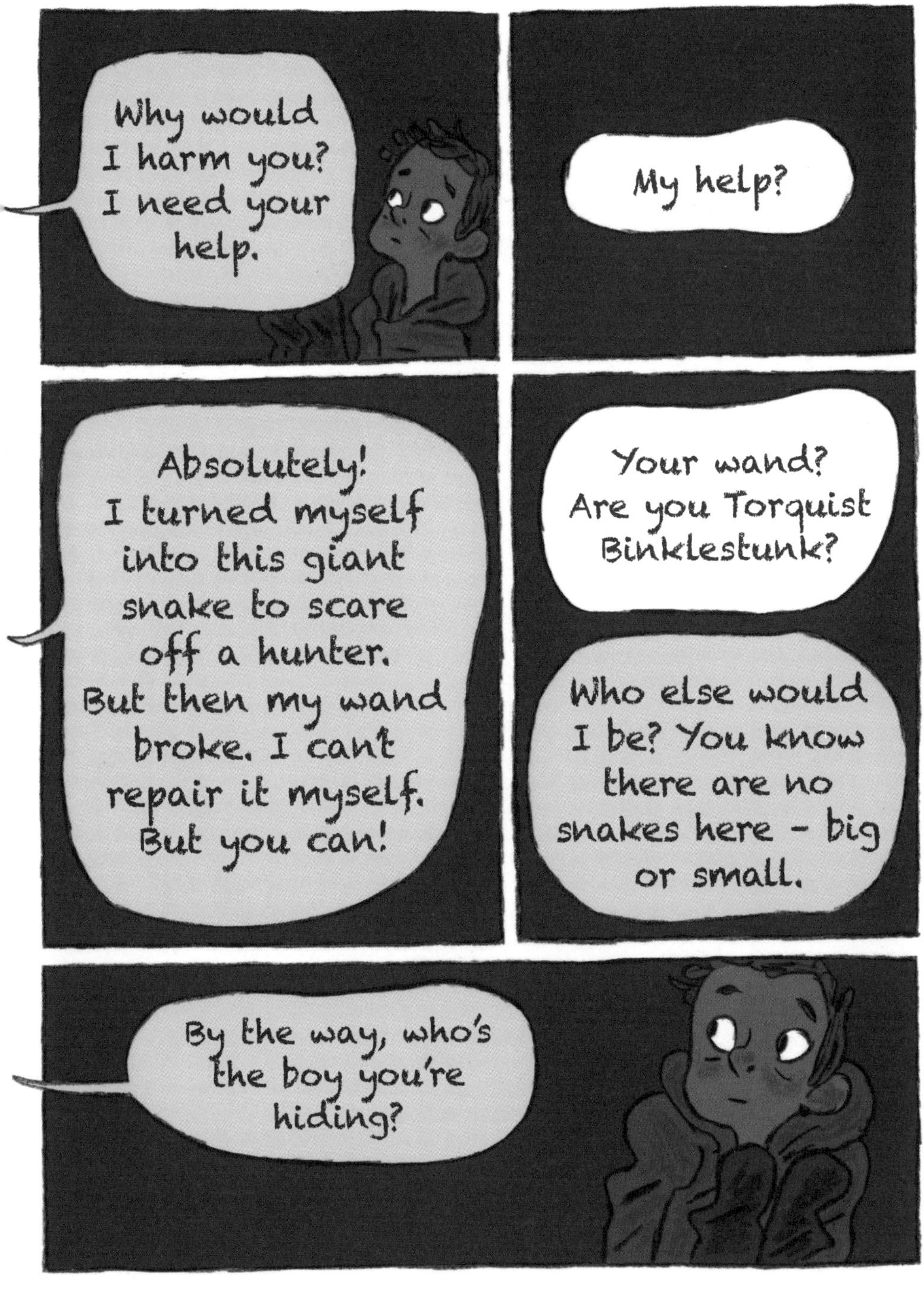
Why would I harm you? I need your help.
My help?
Absolutely! I turned myself into this giant snake to scare off a hunter. But then my wand broke. I can't repair it myself. But you can!
Your wand? Are you Torquist Binklestunk?
Who else would I be? You know there are no snakes here - big or small.
By the way, who's the boy you're hiding?

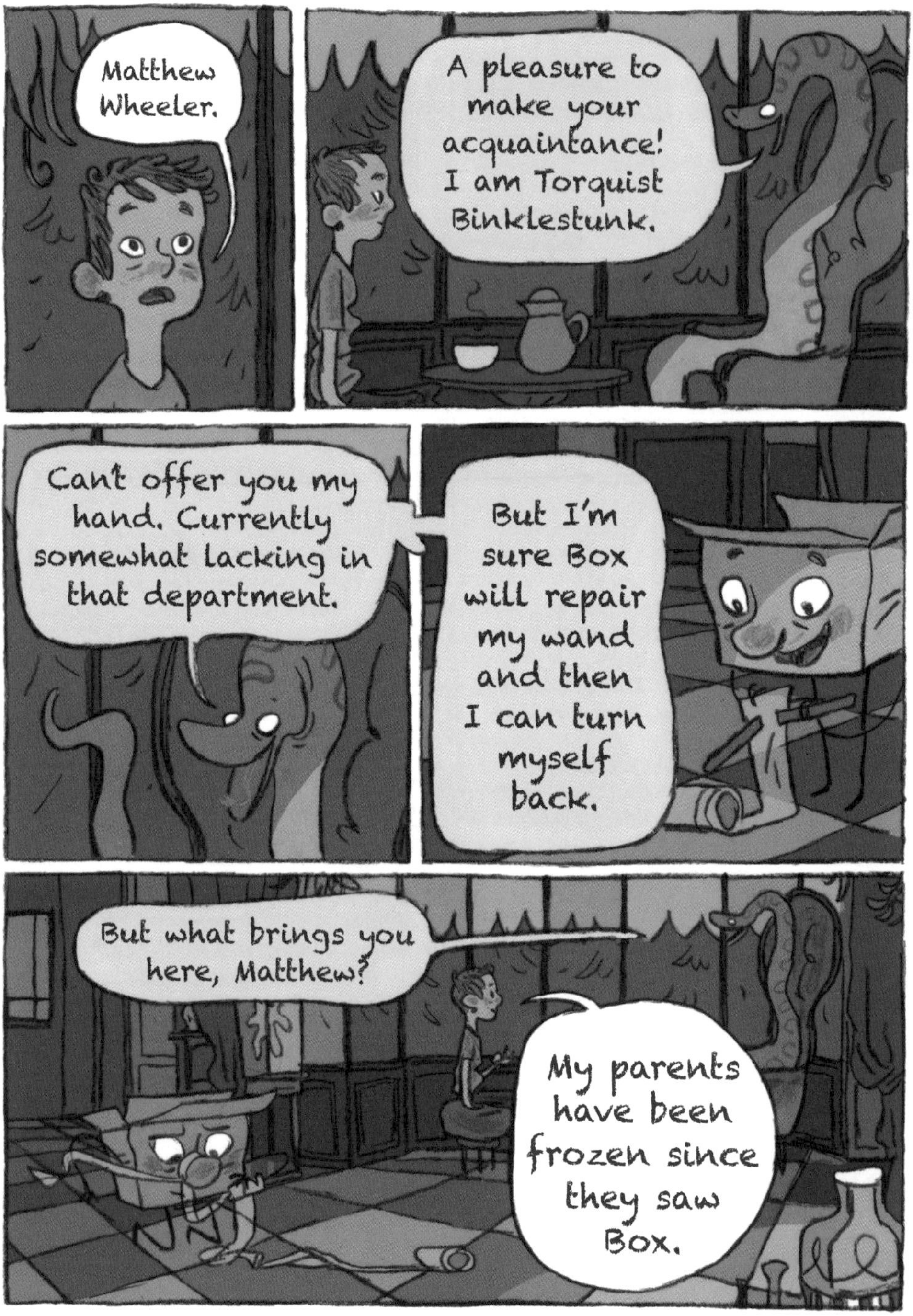
Matthew Wheeler.
A pleasure to make your acquaintance! I am Torquist Binklestunk.
Can't offer you my hand. Currently somewhat lacking in that department.
But I'm sure Box will repair my wand and then I can turn myself back.
But what brings you here, Matthew?
My parents have been frozen since they saw Box.

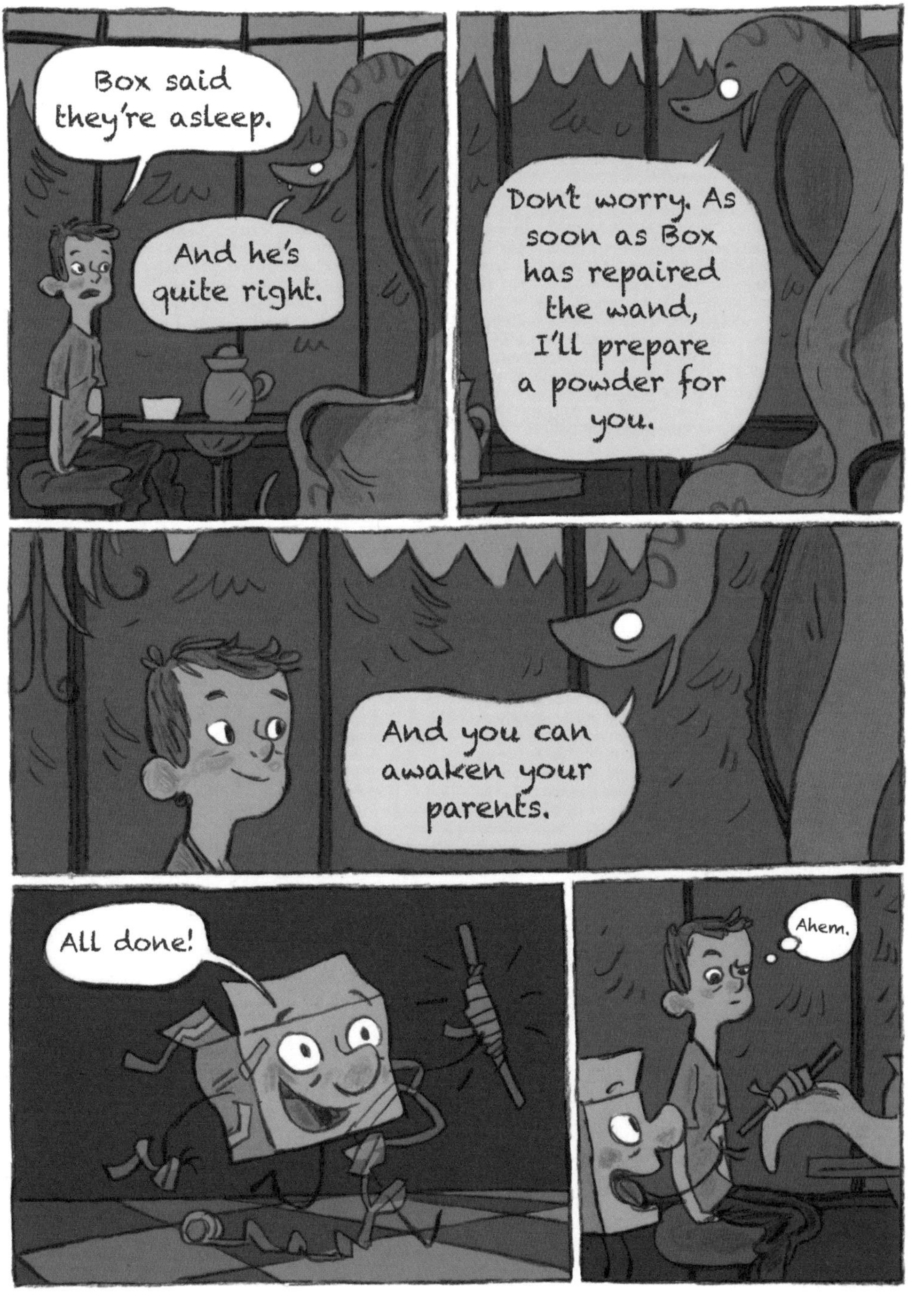
Box said they're asleep.
And he's quite right.
Don't worry. As soon as Box has repaired the wand, I'll prepare a powder for you.
And you can awaken your parents.
All done!
Ahem.

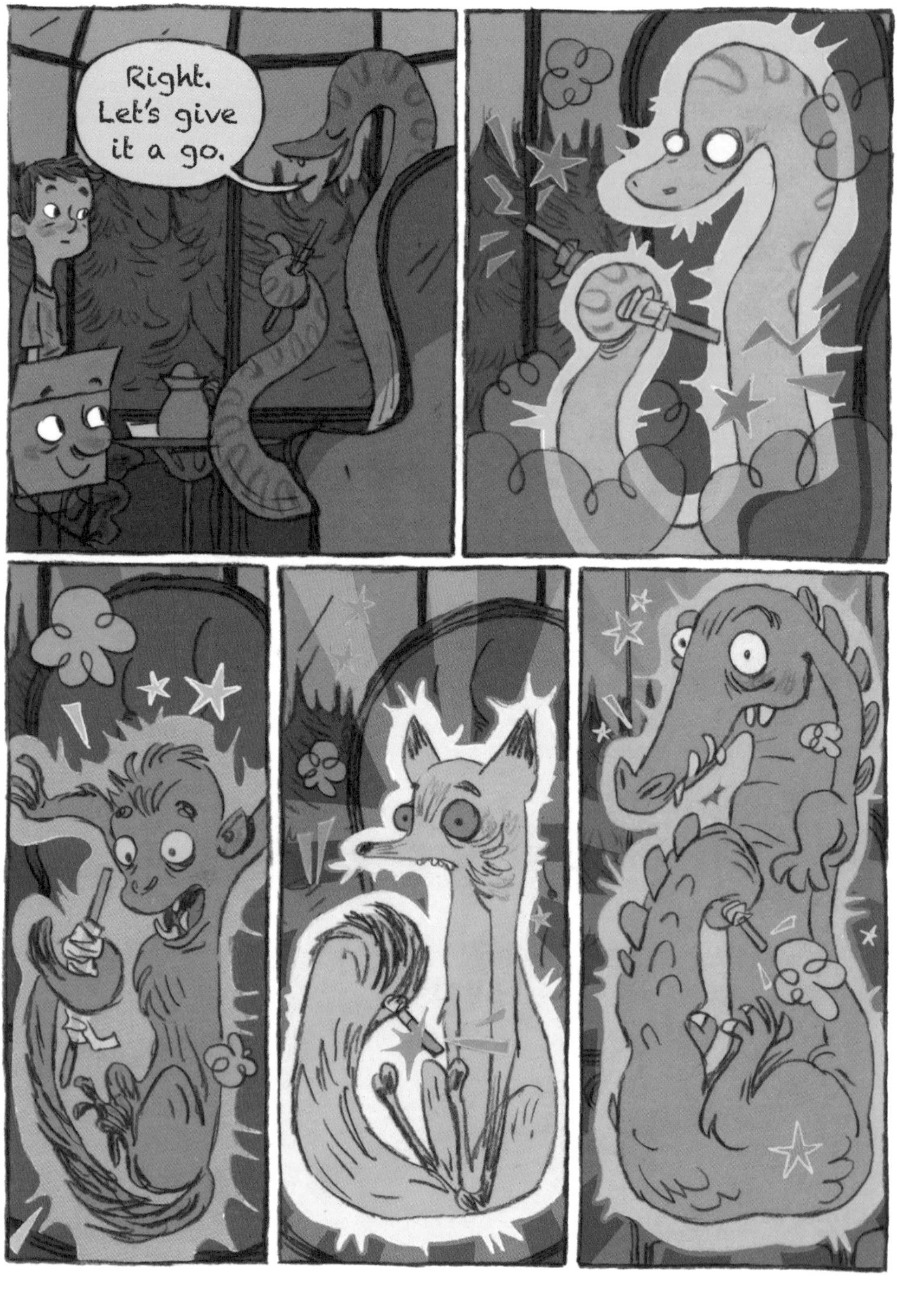
Right. Let's give it a go.

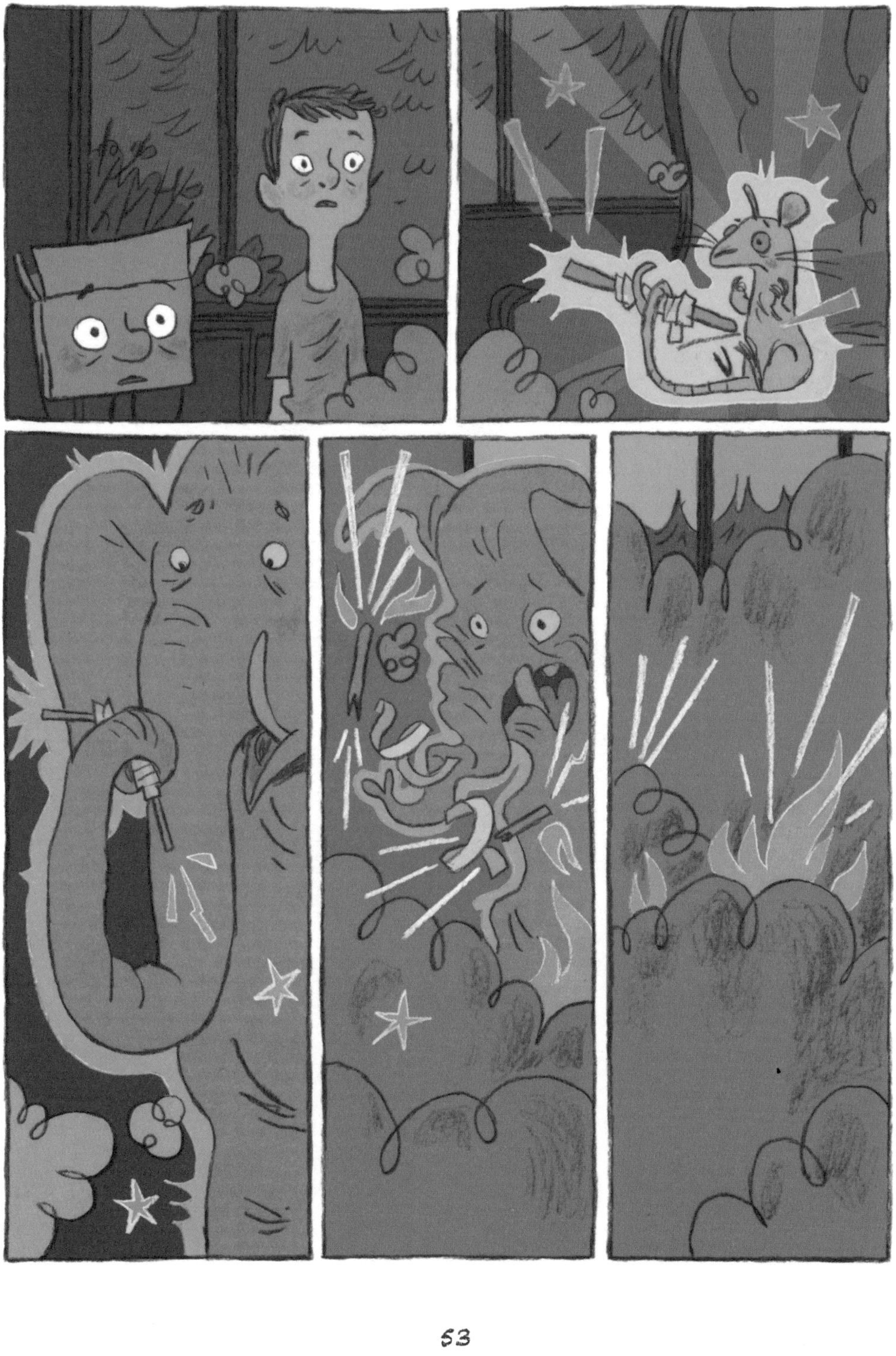

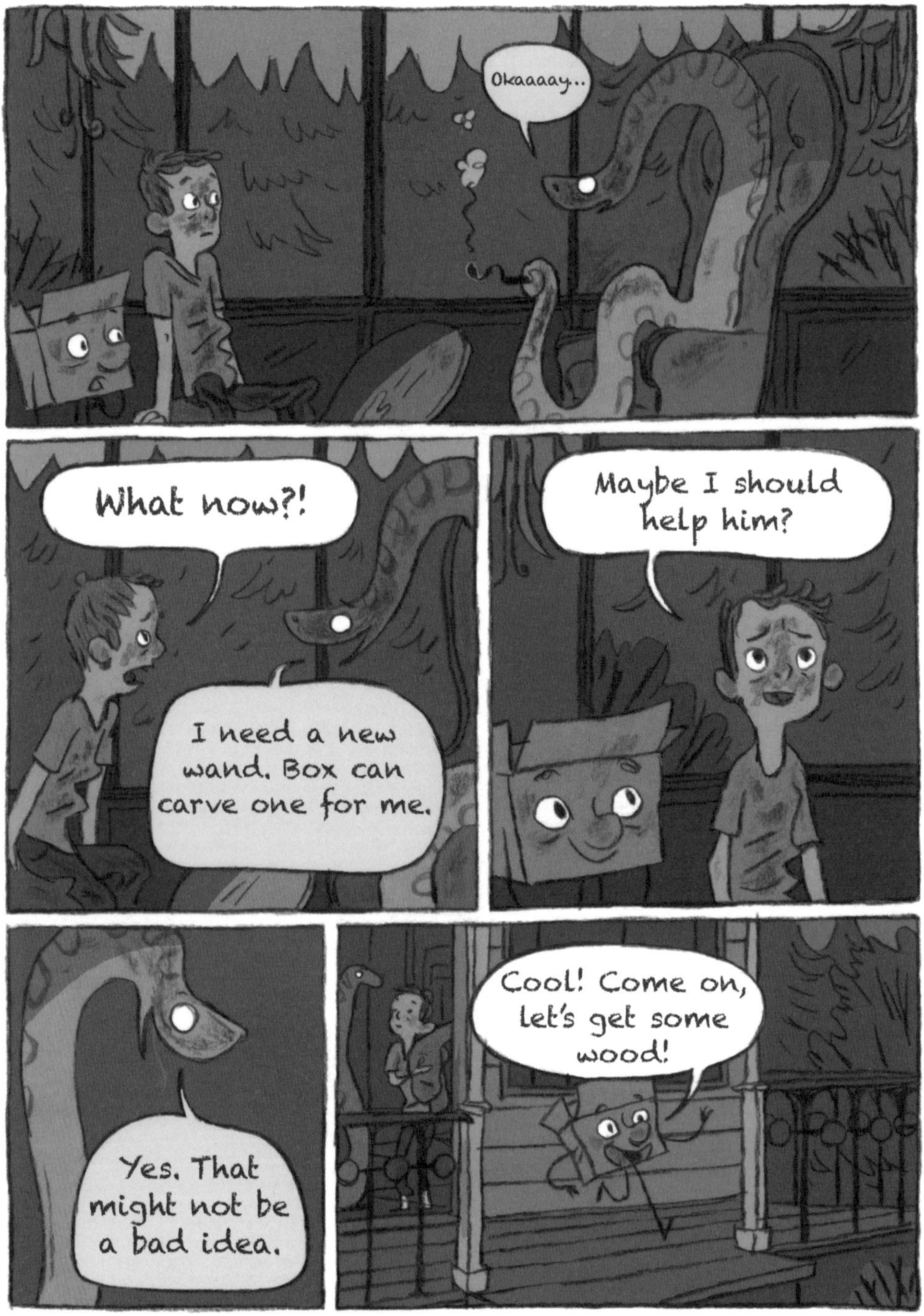
Okaaaay...
What now?!
I need a new wand. Box can carve one for me.
Maybe I should help him?
Yes. That might not be a bad idea.
Cool! Come on, let's get some wood!

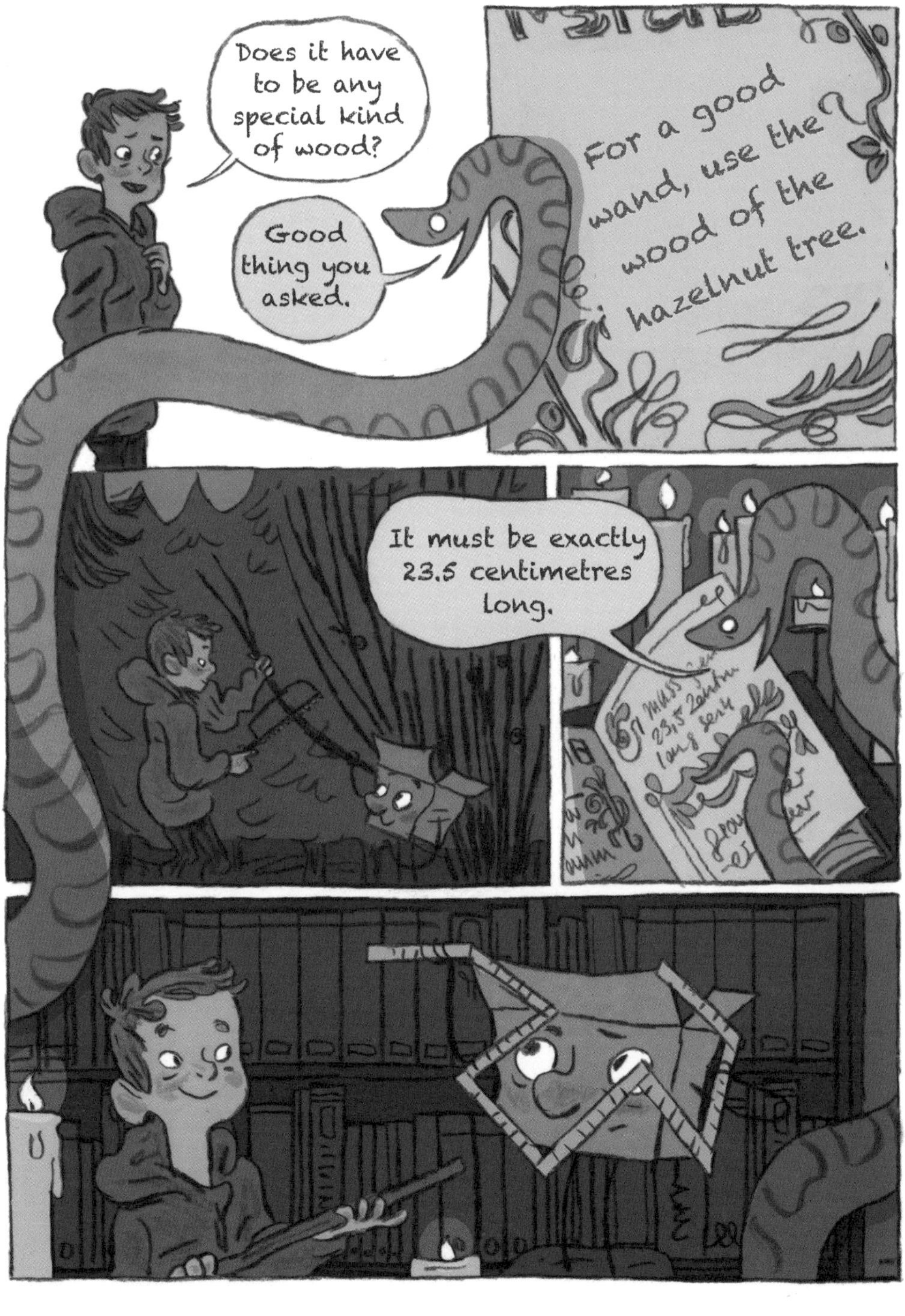
Does it have to be any special kind of wood?
Good thing you asked.
For a good wand, use the wood of the hazelnut tree.
It must be exactly 23.5 centimetres long.

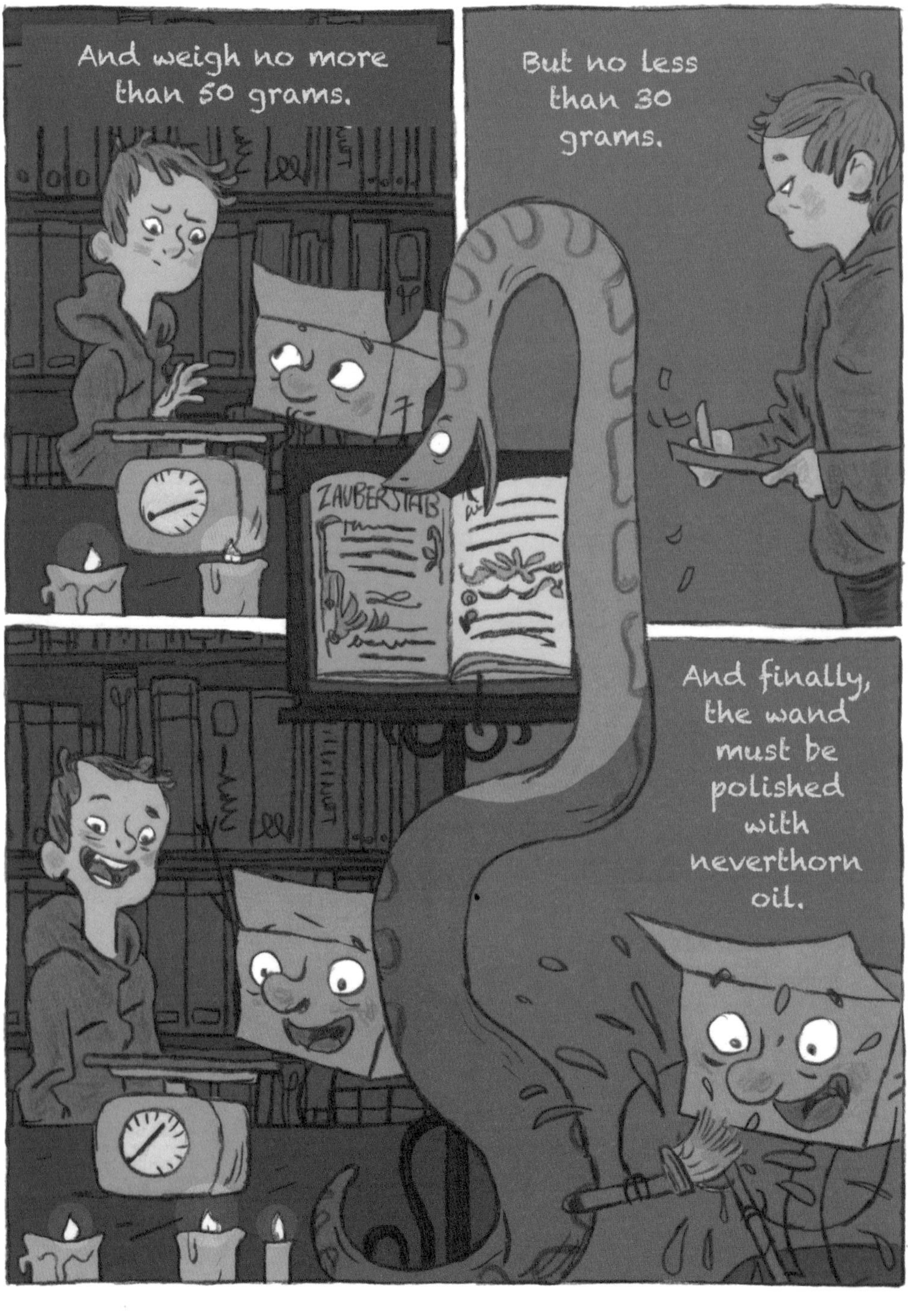
And weigh no more than 50 grams.
But no less than 30 grams.
ZAUBERSTAB
And finally, the wand must be polished with neverthorn oil.

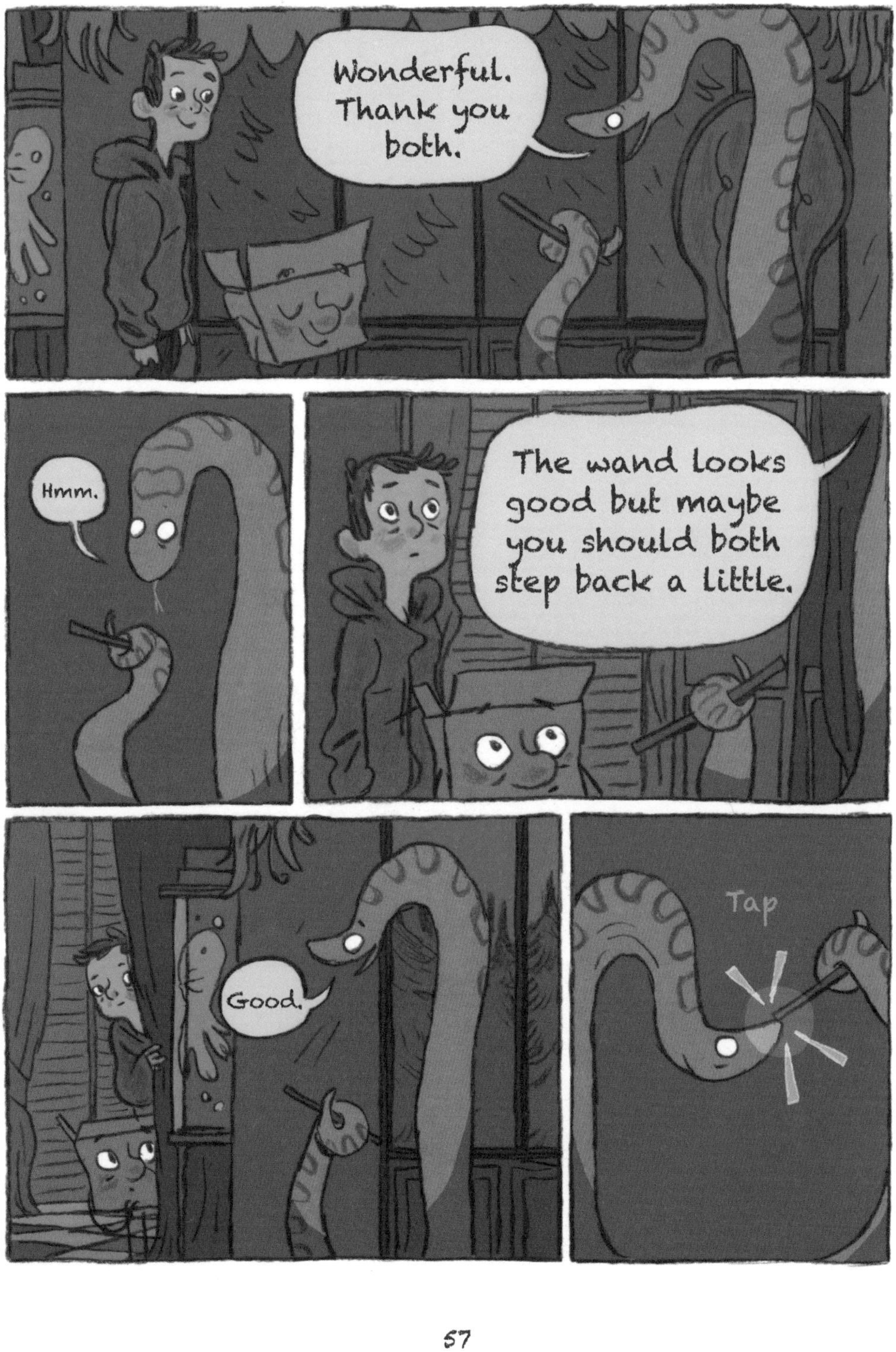
Wonderful. Thank you both.
Hmm.
The wand looks good but maybe you should both step back a little.
Good.
Tap

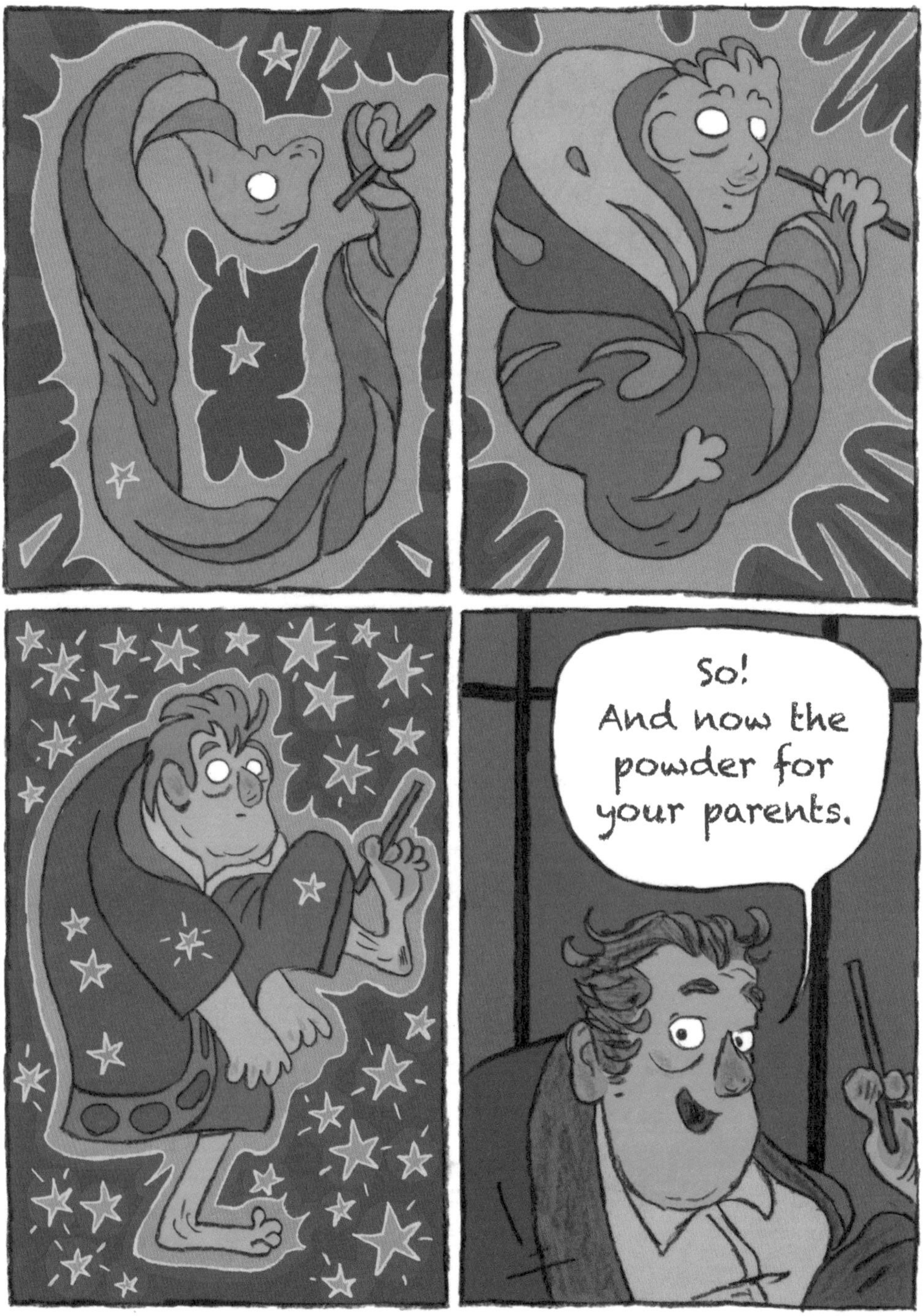
So! And now the powder for your parents.

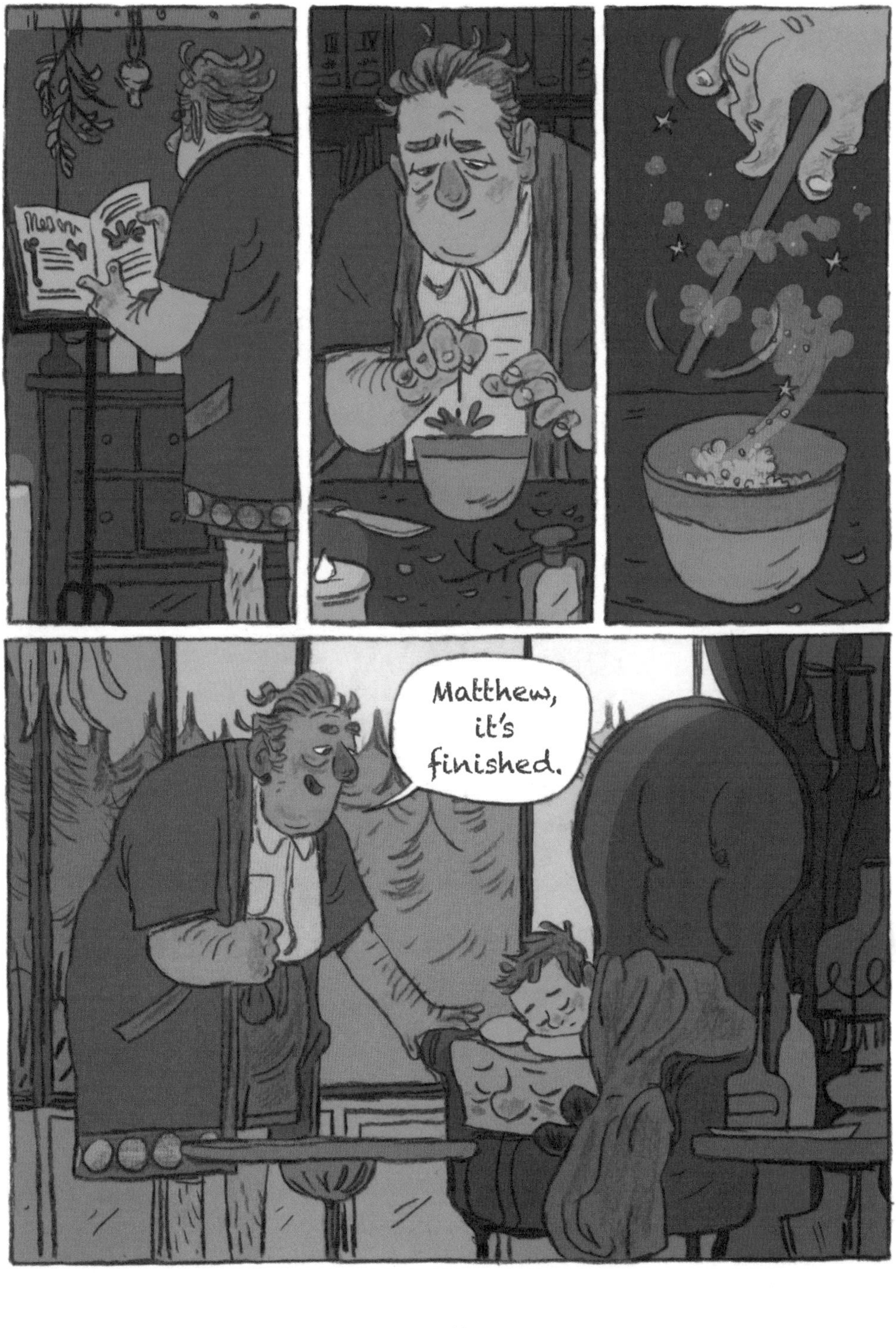
Matthew, it's finished.

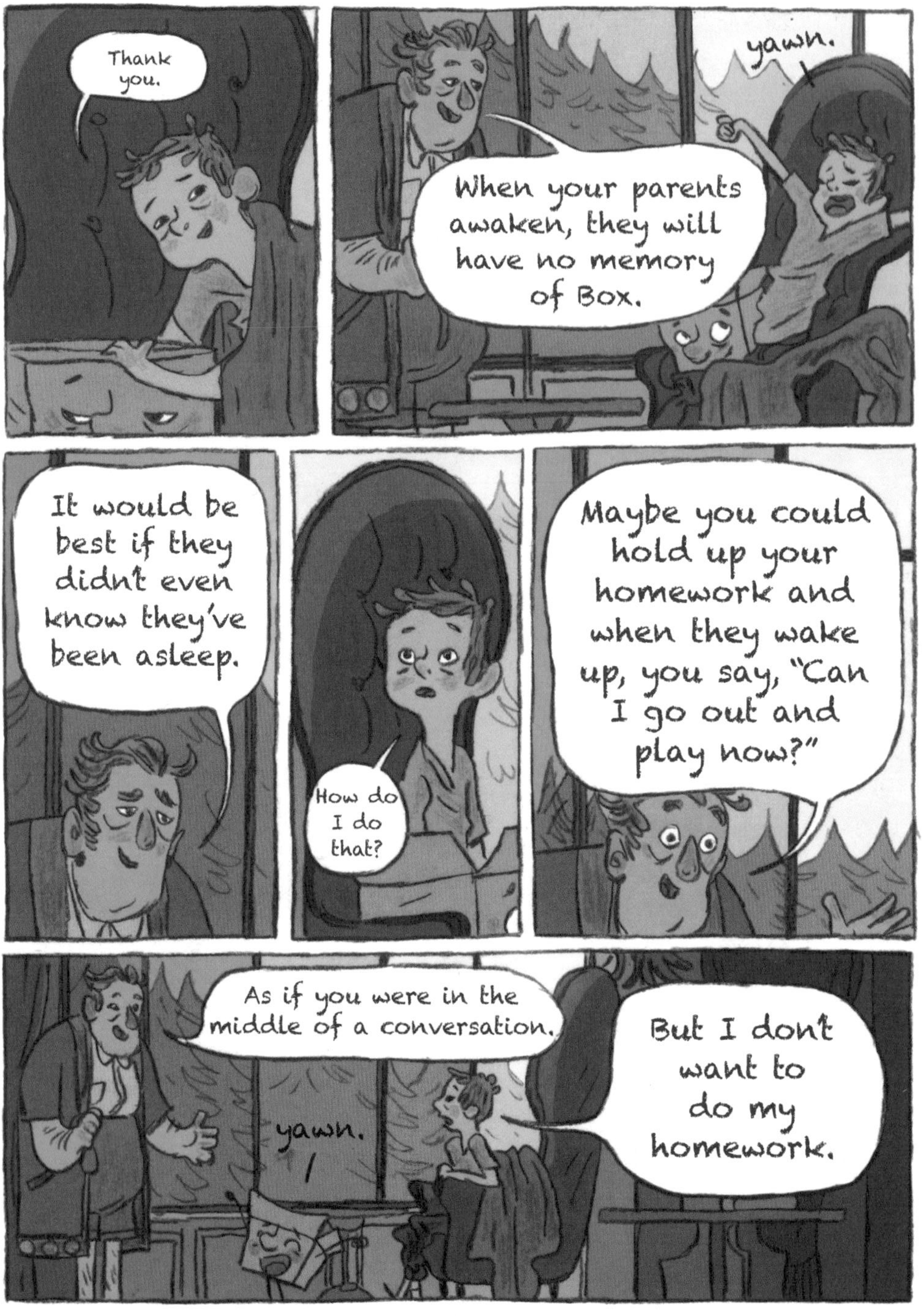
Thank you.
yawn.
When your parents awaken, they will have no memory of Box.
It would be best if they didn't even know they've been asleep.
How do I do that?
Maybe you could hold up your homework and when they wake up, you say, "Can I go out and play now?"
As if you were in the middle of a conversation.
yawn.
But I dont want to do my homework.

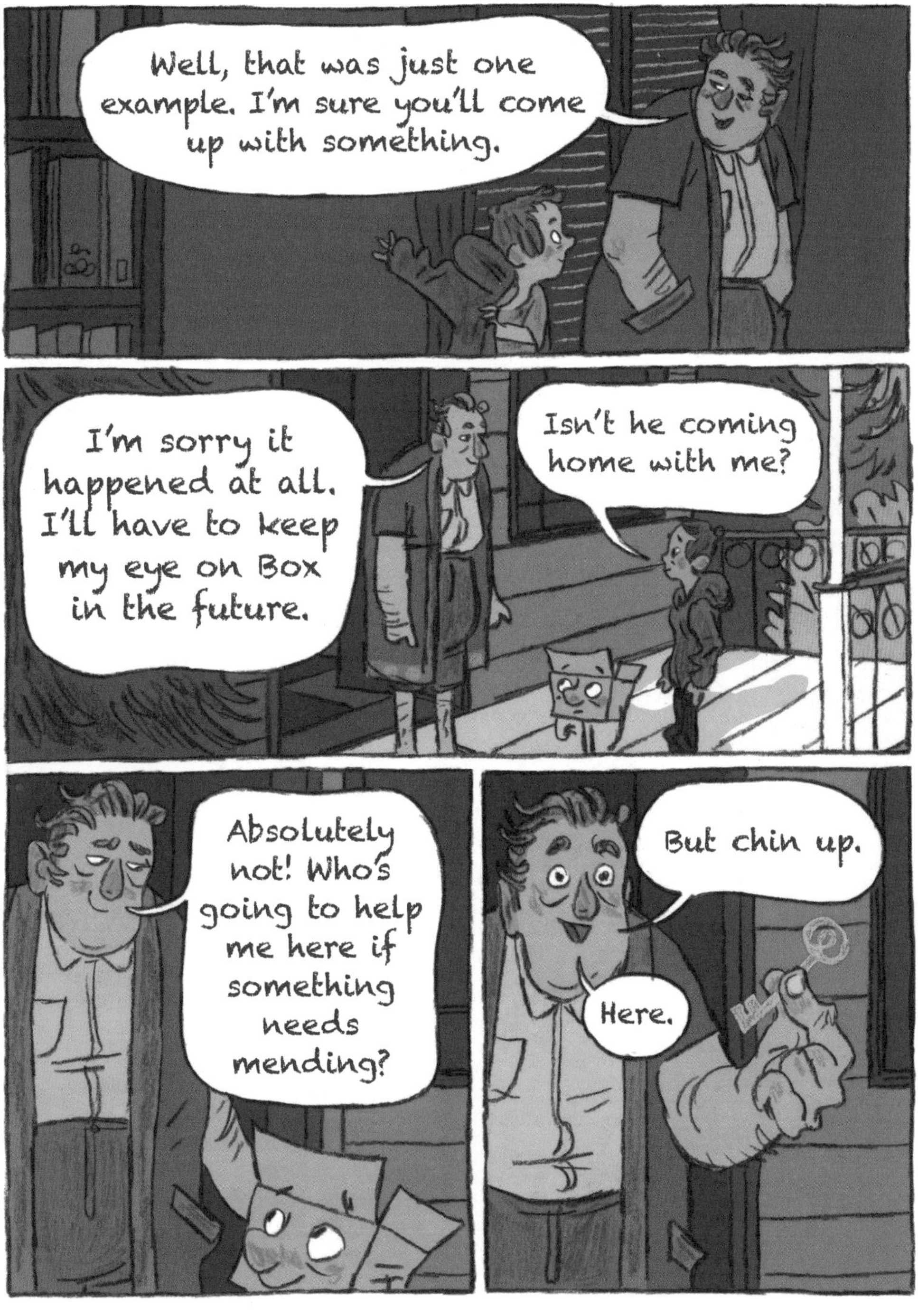
Well, that was just one example. I'm sure you'll come up with something.
I'm sorry it happened at all. I'll have to keep my eye on Box in the future.
Isn't he coming home with me?
Absolutely not! Who's going to help me here if something needs mending?
But chin up.
Here.

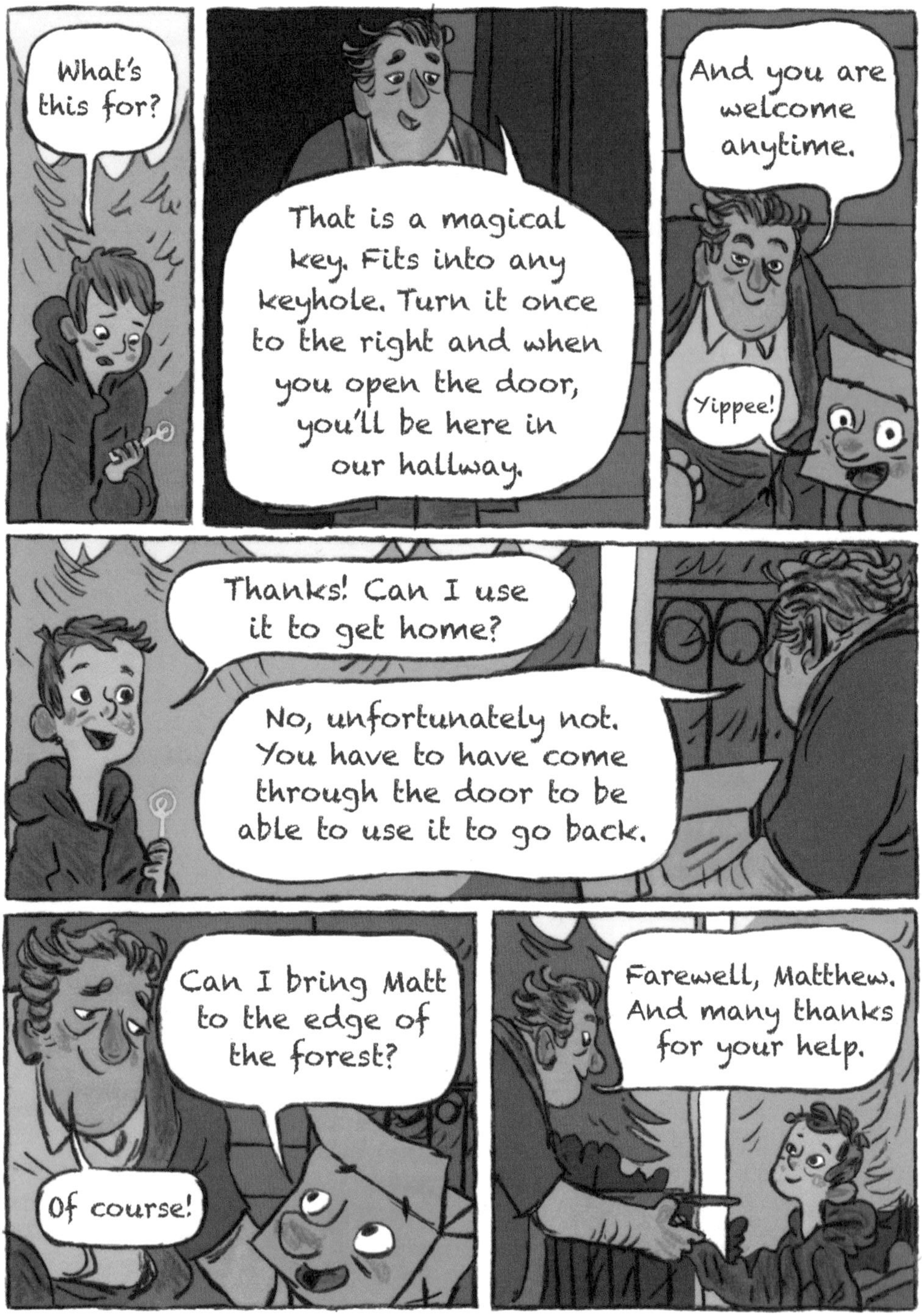
What's this for?
That is a magical key. Fits into any keyhole. Turn it once to the right and when you open the door, you'll be here in our hallway.
And you are welcome anytime.
Yippee!
Thanks! Can I use it to get home?
No, unfortunately not. You have to have come through the door to be able to use it to go back.
Can I bring Matt to the edge of the forest?
Of course!
Farewell, Matthew. And many thanks for your help.

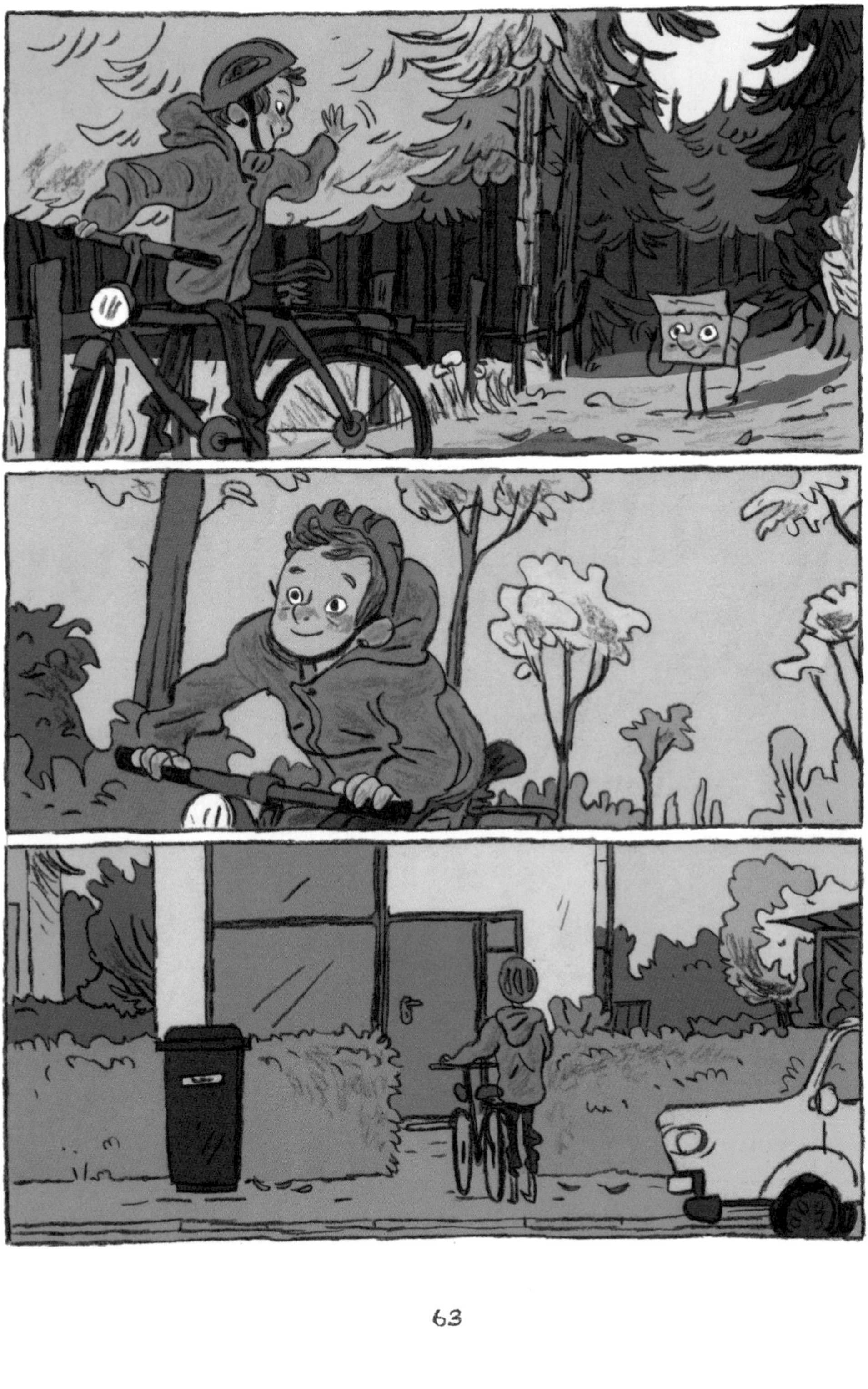

The Awakening

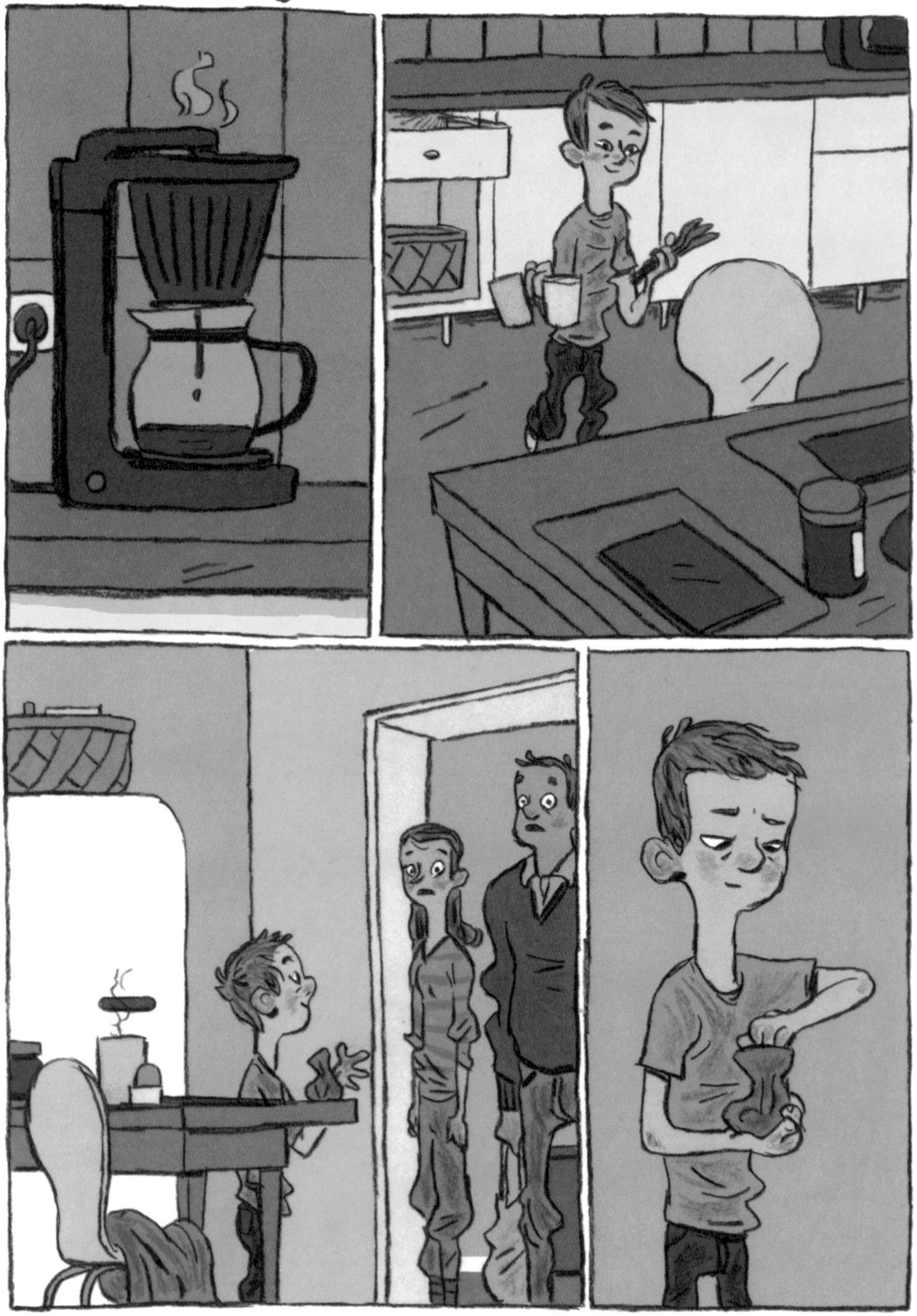

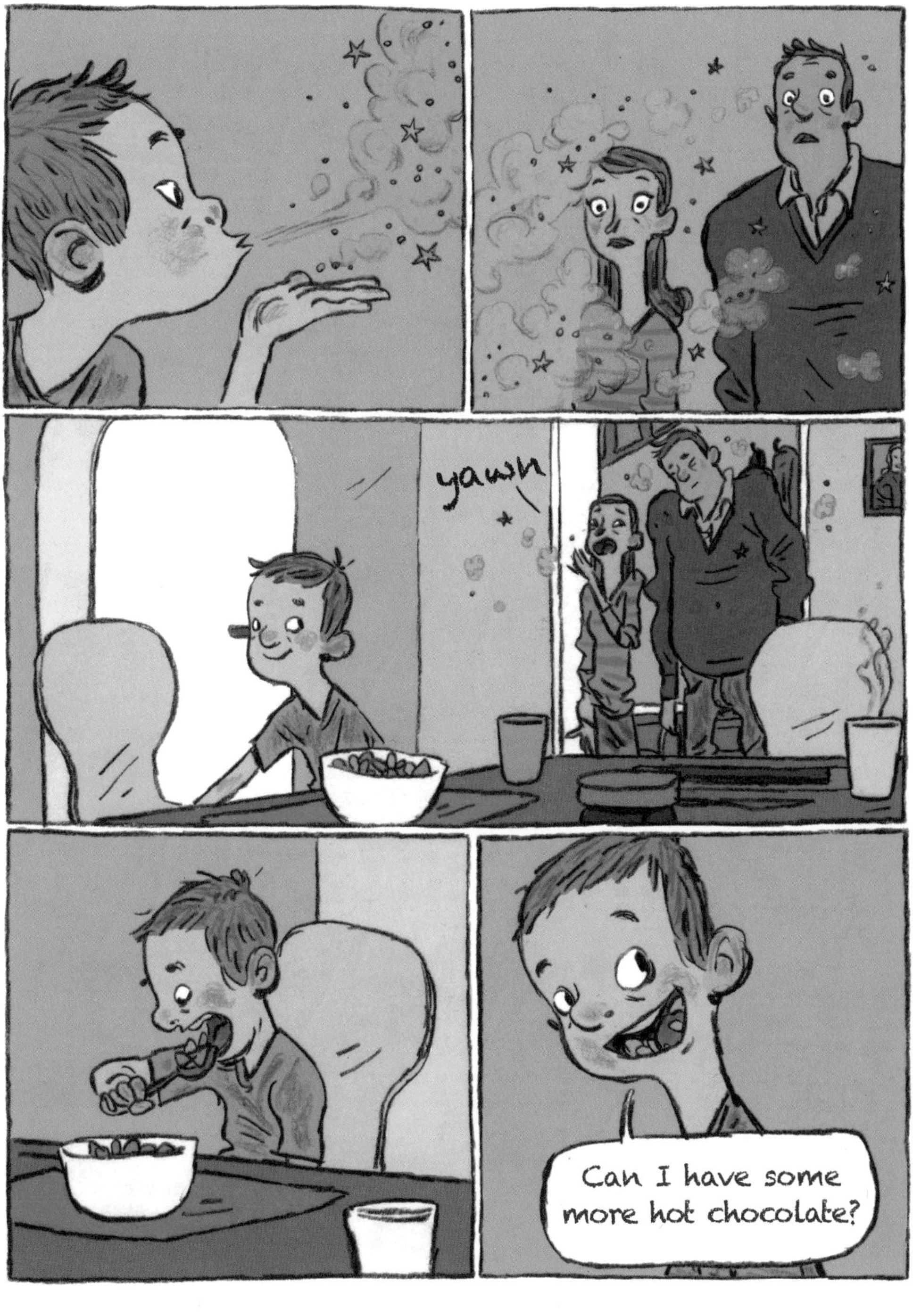
yawn
Can I have some more hot chocolate?

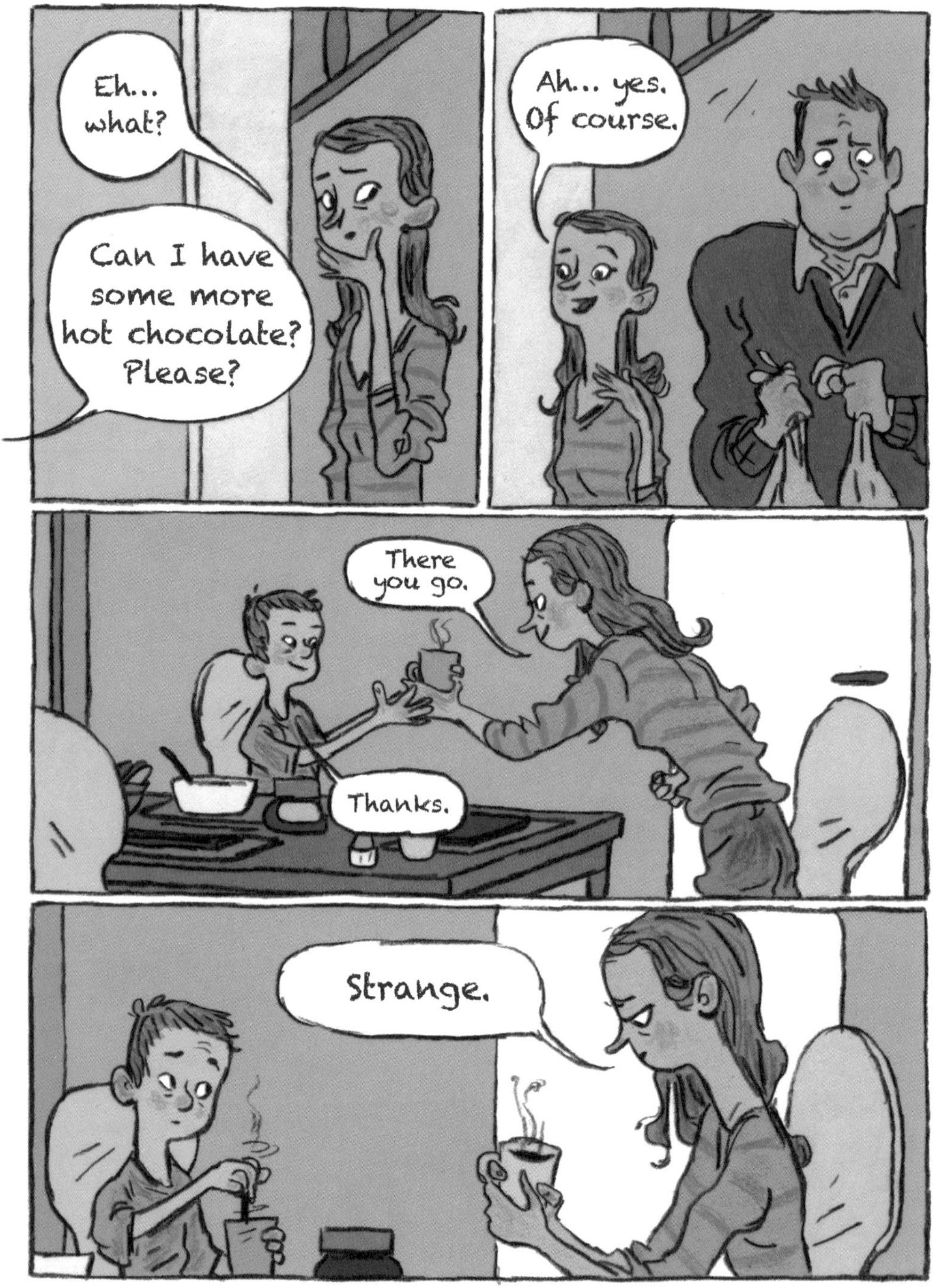
Eh...
what?
Can I have some more hot chocolate? Please?
Ah... yes. Of course.
There you go.
Thanks.
Strange.

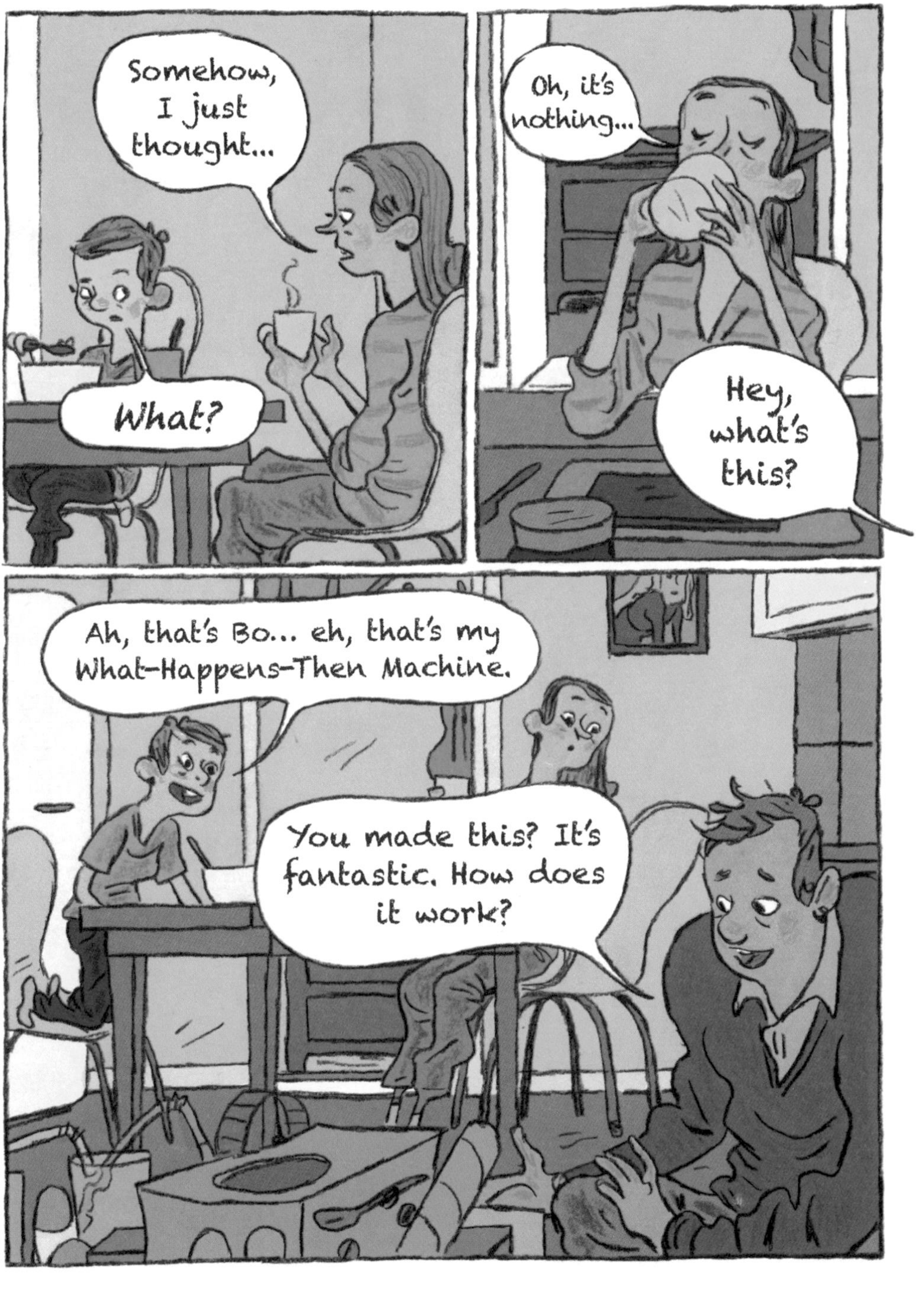
Somehow, I just thought...
What?
Oh, it's nothing...
Hey, what's this?
Ah, that's Bo... eh, that's my What-Happens-Then Machine.
You made this? It's fantastic. How does it work?

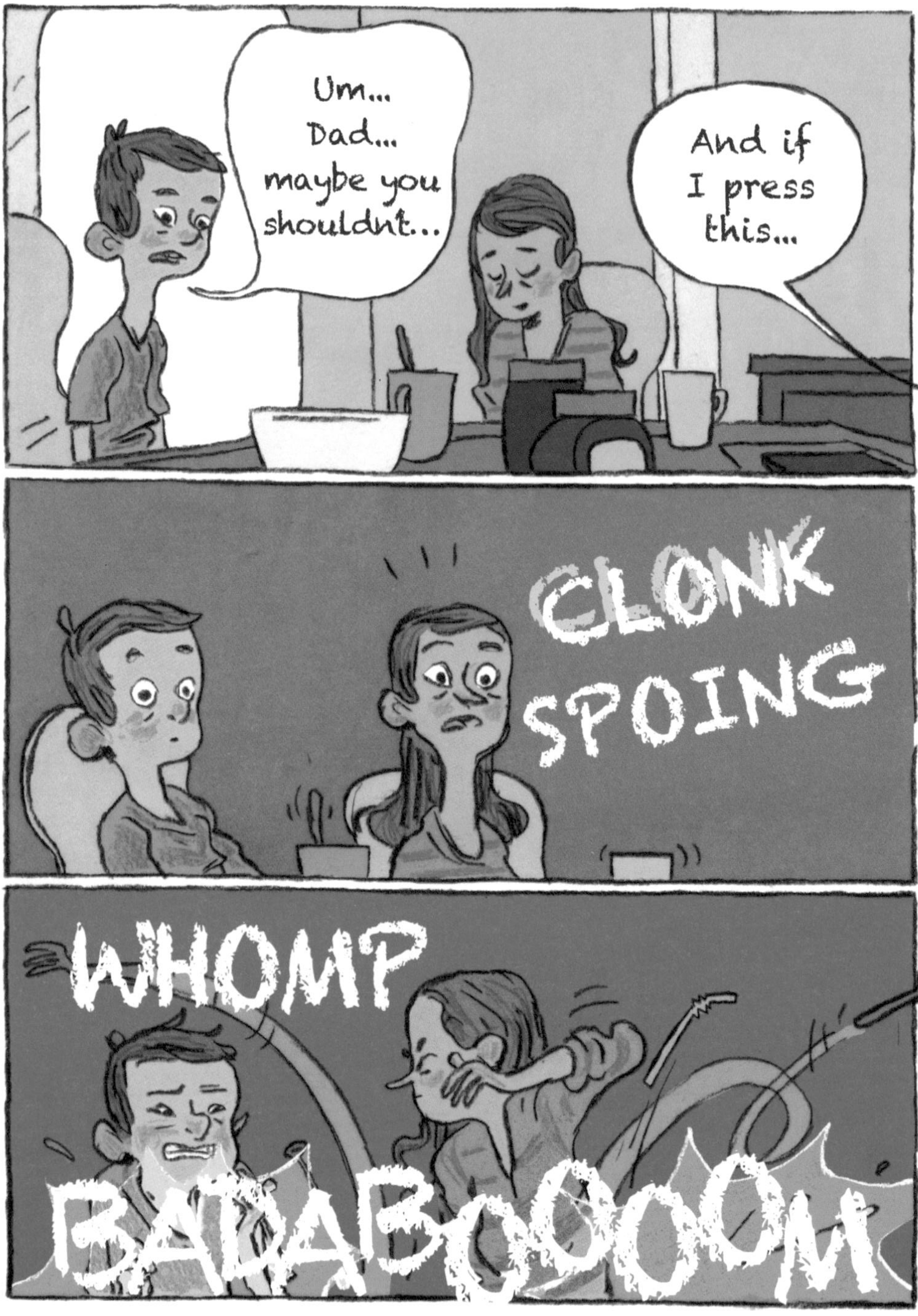
Um... Dad... maybe you shouldnt...
And if I press this...
CLONK
SPOING
WHOMP
BADABOOOOM

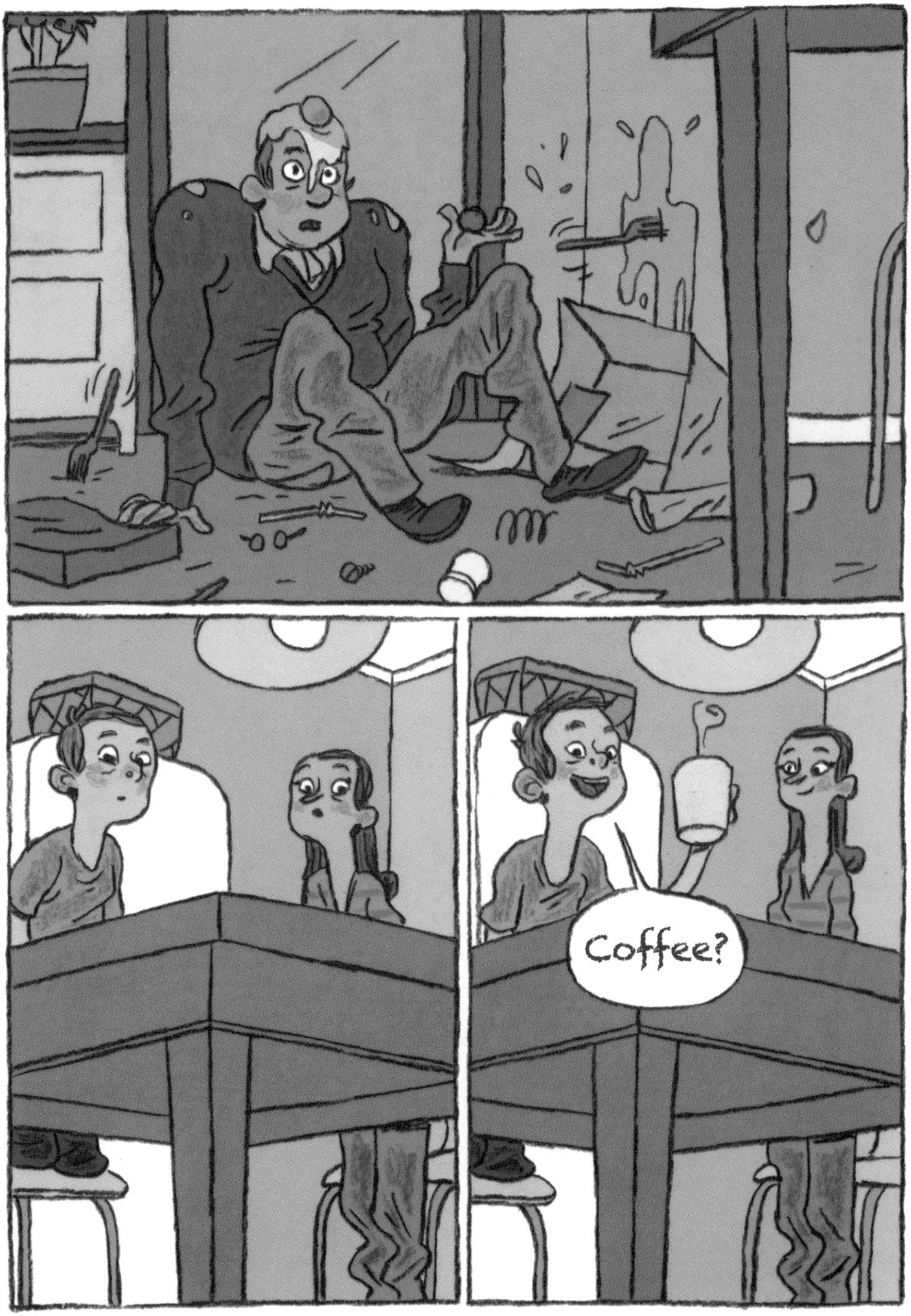
Coffee?